VEGAS
TRYOUT

A PODIUM SPORTS ACADEMY BOOK

LORNA SCHULTZ
NICHOLSON

JAMES LORIMER & COMPANY LTD., PUBLISHERS
TORONTO

James Lorimer & Company Ltd., Publishers acknowledges the support of the Ontario Arts Council. We acknowledge the financial support of the Government of Canada through the Canada Book Fund for our publishing activities. We acknowledge the support of the Canada Council for the Arts which last year invested $24.3 million in writing and publishing throughout Canada. We acknowledge the Government of Ontario through the Ontario Media Development Corporation's Ontario Book Initiative.

  Canadä

ONTARIO ARTS COUNCIL
CONSEIL DES ARTS DE L'ONTARIO

The Canada Council | Le Conseil des Arts
for the Arts | du Canada

Library and Archives Canada Cataloguing in Publication

Schultz Nicholson, Lorna
    Vegas tryout / Lorna Schultz Nicholson.

(Podium Sports Academy)
Issued also in electronic formats.
ISBN 978-1-4594-0071-9 (bound).--ISBN 978-1-4594-0070-2 (pbk.)

    I. Title.
    II. Series: Schultz Nicholson, Lorna. Podium Sports Academy.

PS8637.C58V45 2012   jC813'.6   C2012-900036-1

James Lorimer & Company Ltd.,
Publishers
317 Adelaide Street West, Suite 1002
Toronto, ON, Canada
M5V 1P9
www.lorimer.ca

Distributed in the United States by:
Orca Book Publishers
P.O. Box 468
Custer, WA USA
98240-0468

Printed and bound in Canada.

Manufactured by Friesens Corporation in Altona, Manitoba, Canada in February 2012.
Job #72989

CHAPTER ONE

I stood in front of the notice board and read the audition details three times. Every time I got to the bottom of the page, my knees shook and my heart pounded right through my black tank top.

To be part of a huge show in Las Vegas would be the ultimate, the pinnacle of all my training. The Vegas summer production needed thirty synchronized swimmers, and auditions were being held in Canada and the U.S.

I felt somebody beside me and turned to see my synchro teammate Amy Carter. She was new to the Podium Sports Academy this year.

"Wonder when this was posted . . ." Amy slid a hair elastic off her wrist and tied her long red curls into a ponytail.

"Must have been today," I replied. "I haven't seen it before and I check this board every day."

"Wow." Amy's gaze was focused forward. She was still engrossed in the notice. "It's in three weeks."

"Looks like we're the only pool in Canada holding an audition," I said.

Amy flipped me a glance, excitement flashing in her

green cat eyes. "Can you imagine being part of such a huge show? The costumes alone would be *amazing*."

"Vegas? For a summer? I could take that."

"Maybe I'd finally get a tan." Amy chuckled, a low, sexy rumble that sounded odd coming from her tall, skinny frame.

"It's so hot there in the summer," I said. "They'd *have* to put us up in a place with a pool."

"Ahh. I'd probably just burn and my face would become a freckled disaster." Amy sighed. "Anyway, I bet everyone from everywhere auditions."

"Oh, yeah, that's a given." Visions of all the synchro swimmers in the U.S. and Canada I had competed against year after year crammed my thoughts. "It'll be a real cattle call."

"You stand a good chance," said Amy. "You've won just about every award there is."

"Yeah, but this one will be a lot about looks." I was going to add "and weight," but instead I added, "It's Vegas. And Vegas is all about how you look."

I'd never had the typical synchro body, but I'd always been able to sort of control my weight — that is, until last spring when the doctor put me on the birth control pill to stop my acne. Now my face was clear, but I had grown boobs, a butt, and thunder thighs.

As I turned from the board, I bumped into Wanda Smith, another tall, skinny teammate. Only she was nothing like Amy in personality.

"You guys auditioning?" she asked, as if that might be a crime.

I shrugged. "Thinking about it."

Amy piped up with, "It's a free world." Then she stuck her nose in the air and headed into the change room.

I started to follow but then Wanda said, "I wonder if they have height and weight restrictions." I stopped in my tracks and gnashed my teeth.

I turned and glared at her. "Wasn't listed," I answered with an edge to my voice.

"It's a professional production," she stated. Then she glanced at my boobs. I quickly crossed my arms.

"But then again, it is Vegas and cleavage might work." She laughed, a high, shrill, irritating sound.

Looking down, I saw my cleavage spilling out of the scooped-neck top I wore and immediately uncrossed my arms, letting them hang at my sides. Why had I taken off the shirt I'd had on all day, the button-up one that went over my top and hid everything?

"It's an open audition," I retorted. "I have nothing to lose." Then I turned and stomped into the change room to put on my bathing suit for practice.

Everyone from the synchro team was talking about the audition, and the change room had an unusual buzz. Two years ago I had been picked for Podium Sports Academy, a high school that housed elite athletes from many sports and was in a state-of-the-art complex. The synchro swimmers trained in the best pool in the country, sharing the facility with the swimmers, water polo players, and platform divers.

I undressed beside Amy, hung up my clothes, and put on my one-piece Lycra suit. I snapped the elastic on the bottom and then adjusted the top to make sure I was all tucked in.

"Sometimes I *despise* Wanda." With her nose-clip clenched in her hands, Amy adjusted her bathing cap, tucking her hair underneath.

"Ditto." I also put on my cap and added goggles, which sat on my forehead. Goggles weren't allowed in competition, but we wore them for practices.

"My parents would kill to see me in that show." Amy threw her Mickey Mouse towel over her shoulder. "They *love* Vegas. They go every winter with friends. I just texted my mom about the audition."

I snatched my plain towel off the hook and slipped into my pool flip-flops. "I'm sure my mom would come down too. She'd watch the show a gazillion times."

I dug in my bag for my nose-clip. My father, now, would be a different story. I hadn't talked to him in almost a year, and with good reason.

I looked at Amy and said, "We both have to try."

"Try what?" Wanda barged into the conversation.

I glanced at Amy. She rolled her eyes and shook her head.

"Omigod," said Wanda, "I forgot to tell you." She turned to look at me. "Nathan, that crazy lacrosse player, says you have the best body in the world."

"O-kay," I replied, not knowing quite what to say. Nathan was my friend, so this was weird.

Wanda wound her blond hair into a bun. "He even thinks you would make a great porn star."

I winced, the jab penetrating deep. I'd heard this before. To combat my feelings, I glared at her. "Yeah, right. And I believe you."

"Why would you say something like that?" Amy, her eyes widening, asked Wanda.

"Hel-lo," said Wanda. "It's a compliment."

"Not really," I snapped. "It's hurtful." And it was, big time. My nickname back in Toronto had been Curvy Carrie and I hated it. Now I was even curvier, which totally sucked.

"I didn't mean it to be, honest."

I turned to Amy, ignoring Wanda, and said, "I hope we work on our team today."

"Me too. I love the choreography. You're so lucky you get to be on top of the lift." Amy spoke with no hint of jealousy at all.

Our synchro group had ten swimmers, but only eight were put in a routine, which meant that two were alternates and they rotated with the eighth swimmer. Amy had been an alternate until a few weeks ago when our coach, Susan Harris, had made changes and given her the seventh spot.

I glanced at the clock. "Come on," I said. "We better get to the pool. Susan will kill us if we're late."

Amy and I left Wanda and headed out to the pool.

"I bet Nathan never said that," Amy muttered.

"I know he didn't."

"I bet she's jealous," Amy added.

"No, she's just a bitch."

When I entered the pool, I inhaled, smelling the chlorine. Right away, I felt my body relax. The pool had always been my place to unwind and forget about my dysfunctional home.

Amy and I headed over to the warm-up board to see what the workout was for the day. For the first hour of practice, we usually swam laps that were combined with some synchro moves. Susan was big on cardio. My coach at home in Toronto hadn't been as strict with the cardio, but I didn't mind Susan's warm-ups. They did help improve breathing and strength. I slipped my nose-clip on and had just put my goggles over my eyes when I saw Susan enter the pool area with her clipboard. Our assistant coach, Tracy, walked beside her and was wheeling in the scale.

"Before warm-up we're weighing in!" yelled Susan.

I groaned. Last night, because it was Sunday and our day off from the pool, I had gone out for dinner with my boyfriend, Aaron Wong, and splurged on pasta, and I hadn't gone to the bathroom yet today. If I had known we were weighing in, I wouldn't have eaten lunch. Or breakfast. And I might have taken a laxative. When all ten of us were circled around the scale, Susan said, "Wanda."

Wanda stepped forward and onto the scales.

"One fourteen." Susan wrote the number in her ledger. "Good girl. You've lost two pounds."

"Amy."

Amy stepped onto the scales, wringing her hands. This weigh-in stuff was new to me too, and it was totally random and nerve-racking. If my club coach back home, Mindy Friesen, knew about any of this, she'd freak. She always claimed that size should not be associated with the scale. My mom agreed with her one hundred percent.

Susan smiled at her. "It's one eighteen. You've lost two pounds as well. I'd like to see you lose two more, but that's it, no more after that."

Susan went through every girl before she got to me. I

was last; not good. She always had something to say to the last girl.

"Carrie."

I sucked in a deep breath and stood on the scale. When it was all balanced out, I could have cried.

"One twenty-seven." Susan almost bellowed the words.

I heard the gasps from the girls and a few snickers, and I wanted to jump in the pool so no one could see my reddened face.

"You need to lose at least ten pounds." Susan blew out a rush of frustrated air. "Carrie, this had better change by next weigh-in. You're the shortest girl on this team and now you're the heaviest." She snapped her book shut. "Okay, time for warm-up."

Lap after lap, I swam as hard as I could to get my frustration out. I couldn't cry because Susan had warned us that if you cried in her practices, you were out.

Suck it up and swim, Carrie.

After warm-up, we all swam to the side of the pool to listen to Susan tell us the practice details. We were going over our team routine for an upcoming competition. I got in position, and when I heard the music, I started to scull. Our routine consisted of five different synchro elements as well as musical interpretation. We were about thirty seconds in when Susan's voice sounded from the speakers mounted underwater.

"Carrie, I want your legs higher on the vertical figure."

The music started again. I kept working, sculling, eggbeatering, trying to make the corrections.

When the part in the routine came for our throw, a

move used only by experienced swimmers, I was ready. The trick was to get on top of Amy's shoulders, and when thrust up, I would do a Russian split jump, then land with a dive into the water. I had just made my dive, which I thought went quite well, when I heard Susan's voice loud and clear on the underwater speakers.

"Stop! Carrie, you're not working in that spot. You're too heavy for the girls to lift and you're not getting the height I want. Let's utilize your strength, so take Amy's spot as pusher. Amy, I want to see how you can do with this lift. Let's start from the beginning."

I swam underwater to make the switch so that my teammates couldn't see my face and the tears that were threatening to spill from my eyes.

I took my new position and got ready for the music to begin. All practice I worked and worked to get my legs higher and out of the water more, hoping that Susan might move me back. But my hard work didn't pay off and I stayed where I was.

After practice I quickly got undressed and showered, without saying much of anything to anyone.

I was towelling my hair when Amy quietly asked, "You okay?"

I shrugged but didn't make eye contact. "Yeah. I'm fine. I'll handle it." I shoved my wet suit and towel into my bag.

"You're sure?"

"Positive." I slung my bag over my shoulder and glanced at her. "Hey, I'm not mad at you. None of this is your fault. Susan's right. I'm too heavy."

As I walked out of the change room, my hair soaking

wet because I didn't want to be with the girls any longer than I had to, I ran smack into Susan.

"Sorry," I mumbled.

She put her hand on my shoulder and something about the touch made me cringe and stiffen. I knew this kind of touch well. As if she cared when really she didn't. "I want you to work with Amy," she said. "On the throw."

I nodded but didn't speak.

"I also want to give you a food plan. You need to lose weight but you need to do it properly."

A food plan? OMG. Did she think I was an imbecile? My body stiffened. "I know how to eat properly," I replied, my words clipped. "I've been in this sport since I was seven."

"I'm just trying to help you, Carrie. You've put on weight that you can't afford."

"I know I've put on weight."

"Has your diet changed?"

"Not *that* much." Having a hockey player boyfriend who could eat plates of pasta without gaining an ounce was hard, sure. He ate, so I ate. Plus, for once in my life, I was happy and realized that I actually liked food.

"Perhaps . . . it's hormonal." Susan eyed me.

What was she implying? I crossed my arms. I did not want to have a mother-daughter talk with my coach.

But predictably Susan did, because she asked, "Are you on the pill, Carrie? I've had many swimmers go on the pill and immediately put on weight. There are other methods of birth control."

My cheeks scorched with heat. None of this was her

business. "I'm on it for acne," I mumbled.

Susan gave one of her thoughtful slow nods, as if she didn't believe me. Then she said, "There are a lot of products you can use to help with acne. And makeup covers acne as well. For the sake of the team and for your synchro career, you might want to rethink your options."

"I'll lose the weight."

"All right." Susan shook her head once, clearly not agreeing with me. "I don't want you on some crazy diet, though. You must do this properly."

I sucked in a deep breath so I wouldn't blow up. She sounded like my father. *I don't want you doing this and you must do that.*

"Don't worry." I gave her the phony smile I'd perfected over the years.

"Good. We don't compete at Nationals for three months, so this will give you time to follow a sensible and nutritional food plan if losing weight is what you think you should do. I will email it to you. But, honestly, you could make your life easier if you just went off the pill. The weight will drop in a month's time."

She patted me on the shoulder, then walked away.

I moved quickly down the hallway, my head lowered. I was not going off the pill. I would not, could not, become a red, blotchy mess again.

There was only one way to fix this. And I didn't have three months.

I had three weeks.

CHAPTER TWO

When I got back to my billet, I walked into an empty house. Being alone in the house suited me fine because sometimes my billet parents picked up on my mood. If they were worried about me, then they would phone my mother, which was not what I needed. After putting my backpack in my room, I went into the kitchen to find a note on the kitchen table.

We're at a show tonight, it read. *Your dinner is on a plate in the refrigerator.* The note was signed Mr. and Mrs. Sandford.

Being older, my billet parents liked being called Mr. and Mrs.

I left the note on the table, opened the fridge, and pulled out my dinner. At the sight of the mashed potatoes that went along with the grilled chicken and broccoli, my stomach heaved. Mrs. Sandford always put whole milk in her potatoes and tons of butter, and she whipped them with garlic, and they were the most amazing potatoes I'd ever eaten.

The garbage can stood just two steps away, so I flipped it open and tossed my entire dinner out, making sure to bury it so Mrs. Sandford wouldn't notice and ask me questions. Then I went to my room and sat cross-legged on the bed with my laptop in front of me. I logged on and went directly to my email. Sure enough, Susan had already sent me the link to the stupid food plan she wanted me to go on.

When my cell phone rang, I looked at call display and saw Aaron's name. I quickly answered it.

"Hey," he said. "You want to go out for a bite to eat?"

I had my cell phone pressed to my ear and my computer in front of me as I read what I was supposed to eat every day. Breakfast was the typical boiled egg and dry wheat toast and a bowl of oatmeal with no sugar and skim milk, plus a piece of fruit.

"Carrie, you there?" Aaron asked.

"Uh, yeah, sorry. I was just reading something." I kept reading even though the diet was something I already knew tons about.

"What are you reading?"

"Nothing important."

"We could meet somewhere," Aaron said.

"Uh . . ."

"Are you on Facebook?" Aaron asked. "It that why you're ignoring me?"

"I can't go out to eat." I closed the laptop. "I've got too much homework. I left it all weekend." My stomach growled.

"You want help?" he asked. "I can hop on the C-Train and be there in half an hour."

"Sure, if you want." Maybe Aaron could cheer me up. "But I have to be in the pool early tomorrow."

"I've got early training too. I won't stay long."

In less than thirty minutes, Aaron was ringing the doorbell. I opened it, smiled at him, and sang, "They're not home."

He stepped inside and immediately took me in his arms and kissed me, long and hard, his burning breath igniting something deep inside me. Electricity flowed through me and made my nerves sing. Aaron was my first real boyfriend. When he ran his hand through my hair and pulled me closer, I reached up and touched his face, his skin like velvet. He reacted by spinning me and pressing me firmly against the wall. I lifted one leg, allowing him to move even closer.

His hard body felt good against mine. I kissed him back, holding on to him like a life raft. When our mouths broke apart, I rested my cheek against his chest. Gently, he kissed the top of my head. For some reason, just the tenderness of that little kiss made me start to cry. I had been so strong, hadn't cried a drop, and now it was a like a dam had burst. Susan's humiliating words still stung.

"Hey," he said, his voice a caring whisper, "what's wrong?" He pushed my hair away from my face.

"I don't know."

"Did I do something?" He stroked my hair.

"No. No. It has nothing to do with you." I looked up at him and touched his bottom lip with my finger.

"Then what?" He stared down into my eyes.

"It's just that . . . practice was awful today." My shoulders sagged. "I got moved. I'm not the flyer anymore in our lift."

His brow furrowed. "Is that like being taken off the first line?" After he spoke, he kissed my forehead.

I had to smile. Aaron always related everything to hockey. "Yeah. That's exactly what it's like."

"When are the Sandfords coming home?" He moved his eyebrows up and down. Then he tried to kiss me again.

"Aaron!" I ducked and slid under his arm. I stood with my hands on my hips glaring at him. "I just told you something important and all you want to know is when the Sandfords are coming home. You'd be upset too if you were taken off the first line."

"Okay, that sucks," he said.

"Thank you," I replied.

He grinned and stepped toward me again. "It's your birthday in two days." He circled my body with his arms and nuzzled his nose in my hair. "Can I give you an early birthday present?"

"You don't give up, do you?" I playfully tried to get away from him, but he grabbed me by the waist and lifted me so my feet were off the ground. I struggled to get away. But then he started tickling me. I burst out laughing and ran into the living room with him chasing me.

I had just flopped down on the sofa when my phone rang.

"I'd better get it." I moaned and sat up. "My mom said she would phone at eight and to make sure I answered. She has to give me a minute-by-minute update about her flight times for the weekend."

Aaron sat on the sofa beside me, leaned his head back, and closed his eyes. "You're killing me," he said.

"And my mom is going to kill me if I don't answer."

I picked up my phone from the coffee table. "Hey Mom."

As my mom and I hashed over her travel details, Aaron got up from the sofa and went into the kitchen. I followed him.

He pointed to my books, which were spread out on the table and mouthed, "What question?"

He wanted to know what physics question I was having trouble with. I held up three fingers. We had met earlier that year when we shared the same physics class, and while Aaron had helped me through some tough questions, I'd helped him get past some rough times with his new teammates.

"Okay, Mom," I said. "Just text me everything, okay? Love you."

I pressed the END button on my phone and placed it on the table. Then I stared at my books. "I guess we have to do this." I plopped down on a kitchen chair, pulling one leg under my knee.

Just then Aaron's phone vibrated. He picked it up and fired off a text. Within seconds it beeped again. He turned his back and fired off another text.

"Who's that?" I asked.

He touched my nose with his finger. "None of your business."

I reached across the table to grab his phone, but he snatched it up and held it away from me. "Forget it." He laughed.

I danced with my upper body as I sang, "You and Allie are planning something for my birthday."

He pointed to my books. "You want my help or not?"

"What are you guys planning?"

"If you knew, it wouldn't be a surprise."

"You're no fun."

He ignored me. "Question three is easy."

We worked for half an hour on physics. I was so bored, I could hardly keep my mind on track. I kept thinking about my birthday, which made me happy, and my weight and Susan, which made me angry. The two thoughts were like a ping-pong ball.

Finally, after what seemed like hours, I closed my books and leaned back in my chair. I drummed my fingers on the wooden surface of the kitchen table. "I think I should start doing some extra training, like running."

"Running?" Aaron threw his pencil down. "When would you do that? Your sport fills all your time."

"Lunch hour."

"Don't you swim laps for cardio? That's more sport-specific."

"Runners have great legs."

"So do you." He put his hand on my thigh.

"I have tree trunks."

"You don't have tree trunks." He moved his chair closer to mine, snuggling up to me.

"You want some popcorn?" I said, changing the subject.

He leaned back in his chair. "I can think of other things I want more."

"The Sandfords are going to be home in, like, ten. We can't get caught again."

Aaron pushed his chair back and sighed loudly. "Alright. Let's do popcorn."

I got out the hot-air popcorn maker and butter from the fridge. The feel of the butter in my hands made me cringe. I couldn't, I wouldn't have any. Not even one piece of popcorn with butter on it. Not one.

"Hey, let me help," said Aaron. "I can melt the butter."

Once the popcorn was made, I plopped the bowl on the table and Aaron dumped the butter all over the popcorn. Then he shook it up.

The popcorn smelled amazing, reminding me that I hadn't eaten dinner.

Aaron grabbed a handful and said, "What are you up to on the weekend?"

I playfully punched his arm. "I have a competition. Remember? You said you'd come watch on Sunday when you get home from your tournament."

He held up his finger like it was a pistol and pointed it at me when he said, "Right."

"You forgot."

"Not really. I just needed reminding."

I took a handful of popcorn and placed it on a paper towel beside me. The butter stuck to my fingers and I put them up to my mouth to lick it off — until I realized what I was doing and quickly wiped them on the paper towel. "When do you guys leave for the States again?"

"Thursday. The day *after* your birthday." He tossed a piece of popcorn in the air and tried to catch it in his mouth.

"Hey," he said. "Catch this." He held a piece of popcorn between his finger and thumb like it was a dart. Everything to Aaron turned into a game. Usually I played along.

"I don't want to play," I said.

"Come on. Just because I beat you last time doesn't mean you can't give the game another shot."

"That's not why."

Fortunately the back door opened and we both heard voices. Mr. and Mrs. Sandford walked up the back stairs and into the kitchen.

"Hi, Aaron," said Mrs. Sandford, hanging up her keys. "Are you helping Carrie with her homework again?" She smiled at Aaron. They liked him, thought he was polite and good for my grades, which was true. Since I started dating Aaron, my marks had gone up five percent.

Aaron stood. "Hi, Mrs. Sandford. Yeah, Carrie and I just finished our physics."

"Oh, that's good."

I scooped up my napkin with the uneaten popcorn, knowing Mr. Sandford would ask Aaron about his hockey. They both loved talking hockey.

True to form, Mr. Sandford immediately stuck out his hand to Aaron and said, "Hey, how's the team?"

Aaron grinned as they shook hands. "Great," he said. "We won a tournament in Boston a couple of weekends ago. And we're off to North Dakota on Thursday."

"What did you think of that trade the Leafs made today?" Mr. Sandford asked, shaking his head as if he was disgusted.

I snuck over to the garbage can.

"Did you get the dinner I left for you?" Mrs. Sandford asked me.

I hid the popcorn-filled paper towel behind my back and nodded and smiled at her. "Yeah. Thanks. It was delicious." Then I pretended to pull gum out of my mouth.

As soon as she turned her back to me, I opened the garbage can, threw the popcorn in, and quickly scanned the can. Good. I had buried my dinner enough so it wouldn't be seen by anyone.

Then I shut the lid and asked, "How was the theatre?"

"Oh, it was wonderful. The main actor was so talented. Just a young girl from PEI. But she played all these different parts. I don't know how she learned all the lines."

Both the hockey and theatre conversation continued for a few more minutes until Aaron glanced my way and said, "I gotta get going."

After he left, I said good night to the Sandfords and went to my room to get ready for bed. Stripping down to my underwear, I stood in front of my full-length mirror. I pinched the skin on my upper arms, then grabbed my stomach. How gross. I used to have a six-pack. I stood with my feet together and looked at my thighs touching.

I was fat.

Then I leaned closer to the mirror to check out my skin. I only got the odd zit since I'd gone on the pill. No matter what Susan said, there was no way I wanted my acne back. It had been the worst and I'd already tried all the stupid products she'd suggested. My zits were always the huge, red, pus-filled kind everyone could see. Once I got rid of the zits, I started going out with Aaron. He wouldn't have looked twice at me if I had zits. I snatched a little empty notebook off my table and lay on my bed. I would make a journal entry for every morsel of food I ate.

CHAPTER THREE

Tuesday, November 16, 6 a.m. Egg – 74 calories. Whole-wheat toast – 70 calories. No butter. Total 144.

"Hey, Carrie, slow down!" My best friend, Allie, huffed and puffed beside me, her high-top runners smacking the floor with every stride as she tried to catch up to me. "You heading to the cafeteria for lunch?"

"Nope," I replied. "I'm going for a run."

"Say what?" Allie gave me her famous one-eye-up, one-eye-down, you're-crazy look.

The funny facial expression, combined with Allie's wild black hair, made me burst out laughing. "Stop it. I need extra cardio."

"Girl, you get cardio every day. Doesn't that coach of yours make you swim laps for an hour before every practice?"

"It's not enough." I shook my head. "There's an audition for a Las Vegas show coming up and part of it is a fitness test. I need more."

"Cool! A Vegas audition. Wow." She bumped me with

her hip. "You'll do great. And good for you for running. Gag me. I hate running unless I'm on the court with an orange ball. But it'll really give you a leg up. Ha ha." Allie was six feet tall, so when she jabbed me with her elbow, she hit my shoulder. "Get it? Leg up. That's what you guys do in synchro, right?"

"Ha ha. Bad joke."

"Would you slow down? My legs are twice as long as yours and I'm dying here."

"And twice as skinny. Do the laces up on those big shoes and maybe you'd keep up." I kept moving.

Allie grabbed me by the shoulder, forcing me to slow down, but only for a brief second because we were already at the front door of the school. If I didn't get going soon, I wouldn't go, and this was something I had to do. "Well," I said. "Here I go. See ya."

She yelled after me. "You're crazy, girl, but I love ya!"

There were no paths nearby because the school was on the outskirts of Calgary, and not a lot of houses either, so I ran along this endless prairie road. The clear, cobalt sky was a real 360. Many called it the Alberta Big Sky, and now I got the expression. The lack of trees when I first came to Podium made me homesick because Toronto has awesome trees, especially in the fall when the maples turn red and orange. Calgary poplars turn one colour: gold.

Running is hard for me, and boring, so after what felt like forever, I glanced at my watch and groaned. I'd only been gone seven minutes!

I made up my mind not to look at my watch until I reached a sign that was way up the road. I kept moving.

"Okay," I said to myself. "Forget about the pain and incredible boredom and concentrate on losing weight for the audition."

With my thoughts in place, I got into a more comfortable pace. Soon I reached the sign. Fifteen minutes done. Good enough for the first day, plus if I went much farther, I'd miss next class. I turned around and headed back to the school.

After a quick shower I met up with Aaron in the hallway.

"How was the run?" he asked.

"Boring. But I did it."

He eyed the brown paper bag I held in my hand: my lunch. "You didn't eat?"

"I wasn't hungry after running. You want some?"

"Sure."

I opened the bag, pulled out the sandwich, and gave it to Aaron. "I'm trying to cut carbs." Aaron usually ate half of my sandwich, because Mrs. Sandford always packed me way too much. She insisted on making my lunch even when I told her, over and over, that I was capable of doing it myself.

"You sure you have enough?" Aaron asked. "I already ate three wraps."

"If only I could eat as much as you. Yeah, take it." I held up my still-full lunch bag. "There's tons more in here for me."

"Great, thanks. Hey, we're going to be late for next class. I'll call you later tonight. It's your birthday tomorrow." He smiled mischievously.

"Okay," I replied. "You're up to something."

He pointed to his watch. "Gotta go. Mr. Whyte shuts the door if you're late."

Neither of us liked PDAs, so our goodbye did not include a kiss. As we went in separate directions, I almost skipped, thinking that he must have bought me a present.

As I hurried to class, I opened my lunch bag, pulled out the bag of cut vegetables, the apple and plum, and chucked the rest, a few cookies, in the garbage.

Because I was a few minutes late for class, I slunk into English and took a seat beside my friend Nathan Moore. A lacrosse player, he was dressed in his usual tattered jeans and oversized sweatshirt. He turned when he saw me and gave his cool one-finger wave and classic wink. His unruly blond hair flopped over his eyes.

"Hey, Scary Carrie," he murmured.

"What'd I miss?" I whispered. Nathan had given me the nickname last year because I had tapped him on the shoulder in math class, not realizing that he was sleeping, and had scared the crap out of him.

"Same ol', same ol'." He slouched further down in his seat. "He's still droning on about that Macbeth guy."

"Go back to sleep," I whispered.

He gave me a thumbs-up and closed his eyes.

From the opposite corner of the room, I saw Wanda staring at me. I wondered why, and suddenly her words from yesterday about Nathan saying I'd make a great porn star flooded my brain. I crossed my arms over my chest. Some of the lacrosse guys were known to say things like that about girls, but Nathan wasn't like that. At least not around me. But maybe around others? No.

It just didn't seem like him.

My stomach talked, telling me it was hungry, so I pulled out the baggie of vegetables. Mostly cucumbers, which didn't have a lot of nutrients — or a lot of calories. Mr. Carruthers droned on and on, and taking my cue from Nathan, I slouched in my seat. As I quietly munched, I so hoped that my breasts would shrink when I lost the weight. Last year I had seriously thought about getting breast reduction surgery and had talked to my mom about it, but she had been horrified. And that's when I had been skinnier and not on the pill.

Finally class ended and I stood up to leave. I shoved my uneaten plum in my backpack.

"What's shakin', Scary Carrie?"

This time it was my turn to jump. Nathan had come up behind me.

"No fair," I said, putting my hand to my chest. "*You* scared *me.*"

"I just hope you're not thinking about that dude Macbeth."

"I haven't started my paper yet. Have you?"

"Nah. It's in the hands of Coles Notes." Nathan spoke in his usual easygoing way. "Those dudes, they speak a strange language. I wonder if they ever really talked that way in England."

"I don't think Shakespeare'd write the words if they didn't." I tossed my backpack over my shoulder.

Nathan and I walked out of class together. "Hundreds of years from now," I said, "kids will probably think the language in our books is strange too."

"Scary Carrie, you always have an answer."

I changed the subject. "So when's your next game?"

"Friday." He quickly shuffled his feet, pretending he was playing.

"You're crazy." I playfully slapped him on the back.

"Gotta practice my moves." He kept shuffling.

"Some of those guys you play against are so huge. Don't you fear for your life when they're coming at you?"

"Hey." He stopped his crazy movements. "I'm growing," he said. "They don't call me Hulk for nothing." He came to a standstill in the hallway and flexed his skinny arms, puffing his cheeks out and scowling fiercely.

"Stop it. You're turning purple!" I was laughing so hard, I had to bend over at the waist and grab my sides.

Suddenly I felt someone's eyes on me. I straightened and, sure enough, when I glanced behind me, Wanda was staring at me again. Man, she was giving me the creeps. I decided to confront Nathan about what she had said.

"Come on." I pushed him forward. "We better get to next class."

After a few strides I blurted out, "Did you say anything to Wanda about me?"

He frowned but didn't break stride. "Wanda who?"

"You know Wanda. She's in our English class. She's in synchro with me."

"The skinny blond chick?"

"You honestly don't know her? She told me you said something about me to her."

"Um, I've never actually talked to her before. What did I supposedly say?"

"If you didn't say it, then it doesn't matter."

My school day ended and I headed to the pool for practice, munching on my plum, taking small bites to make it last longer. The run had made me hungrier than usual.

"Hey Carrie," said Amy, catching up with me.

I slowed my step. "Hey."

"Susan wants me to work with you." Amy avoided making eye contact. "We have the provincial competition this weekend and she's keeping me on top."

Something pinched me, deep and hard. How could Susan do this to me? I had thought that at least I would have been allowed to be the flyer this weekend. I had been practicing for weeks now. And my mom was coming too, and I'd told her all about it. Now what would I tell her?

"Before warm-up," I said, "I'll go over it with you."

I helped Amy. Susan didn't say thanks, but I didn't care. I worked as hard as I could in practice and did everything Susan told me to do without a grumble or complaint. Every correction I made right away. After practice, I took my shower and got dressed. To my dismay, Wanda was beside me in the dressing room.

"You and Nathan are always together," she said. "Doesn't Aaron get jealous?"

I threw my towel on the bench and turned to glare at Wanda. "What is your problem? Why did you lie about Nathan? He says he's never talked to you. In fact, he doesn't even know who you are."

Wanda's face fell. A little part of me actually felt some pity for her. She had few friends.

"You're such a bitch, Wanda," Amy declared from my other side. Obviously she didn't feel the same pity. "Why do you always have to lie about everything?"

Wanda's demeanour immediately changed. "I can get you taken off the top, you know, Amy."

I froze. All my pity disappeared. I narrowed my eyes and stared directly at Wanda. She met my gaze coolly. "Did you talk to Susan to get me taken off the top?" I asked.

"Nope," she retorted, enunciating the *p*. "I didn't need to. You stepped on the scale and did it *all by yourself.*" Wanda slung her designer tote over her shoulder and with a stupid, evil smile strutted away.

"I think I hate her," I said.

"She's always in Susan's office." Amy grabbed her towel off the hook and threw it in a plastic bag, which she shoved in her backpack. "I saw her there yesterday whining about something."

"She is such a suck-up. Sad thing is, Susan buys into her. I would never suck up like that. My coach back home never played favourites."

"Mine did a bit." Amy pulled on her Uggs. "Such is life. When I complained, my parents always said work hard and it will pay off. And look, it did, here I am at Podium. And the swimmer my coach liked best didn't get invited. Ha ha. That was one sweet moment." She held up her hand. "Bottom line, girlfriend, we don't need Susan for Vegas."

I slapped her hand. "You got that right."

On the way home from practice, with Wanda's words about my weight still stinging, I made a detour and went to Walmart. I went directly to household goods and stood in front of the scales. There were a lot to choose from, but I picked the cheapest one. Then I went to the food section and started throwing anything that was super low calorie, like sugar-free Jell-O, which had just ten calories per package, and the sugar substitute Splenda, into my basket.

I was walking to the cash register with a heaping basket when I heard Allie's voice an aisle over. I stopped. I couldn't let her see me with this stuff; she'd freak. Allie hated it when athletes ate crap. I hid behind the shelves.

"We have to get that!" Allie howled in laughter.

Then I heard Aaron's voice. "She'll be so embarrassed."

"Oh my gawd, it's too funny."

"Come on, let's go pay and get out of here."

I giggled. Aaron hated shopping. I followed from a distance, hoping to get a glimpse of what they were buying, but I couldn't see much.

Once they'd paid and left the store, I approached the cashier and paid for my stuff. Then I headed home. I was just pulling into the Sandfords' driveway when my phone vibrated. I parked, switched off the engine, and answered the call.

"Hey," said Aaron. "I've found a great spot to take you for dinner tomorrow night."

"O-kay." I replied. Weird. Why were they buying that stuff at Walmart? Were they going to embarrass me at school?

"I'll pick you up at the Sandfords' at seven?"

"Sounds good. Is this like . . . a fancy place?"

"I think so. My billets recommended it."

"So what do I wear?"

"Business casual."

I started laughing. "Business casual? What are you — a businessman?"

"That's what our coach calls no jeans."

When I hung up the phone, I sat in my cold car for a minute. Dinner meant good food. Okay. So tomorrow, I wouldn't eat all day.

CHAPTER FOUR

*Wednesday, November 17, 6 a.m. B-day. 126 pounds. Lost a
pound. Only ate 1030 calories yesterday. Ticked off. Wanted to
be down at least two.*

"Happy Birthday!" Allie leaped out at me from around the
corner as I was leaving the pool after morning practice.

I swear I jumped high enough to dunk a basketball.
"OMG, you scared the crap out of me. But thanks for the
b-day wishes."

She eyed me. "What's the matter, girl? You should be
happy."

"I'm happy. Just tired after practice. Susan worked us
hard to get us prepared for our figures competition tomorrow. We had to go over every figure a zillion times."

"You need food." She looped her arm through mine.
"I'm taking you for breakfast. My treat. We both got a spare.
Whole-wheat pancakes, strawberries, whipped cream." She
licked her lips. "We can go to Nellie's. I've got wheels."

"I can't. I just ate."

"You kidding me? Come on."

"Compromise. How about Starbucks?"

"You're no fun, but it is your day and you get to pick the place. Let's go."

Allie ordered a latte and muffin and I got a green tea. Over the rim of her paper cup, Allie smiled, her chocolate-coloured eyes dancing. "I know what Aaron got you. You are gonna love it."

"What is it?" I leaned forward.

"I'm not telling. Have you talked to him yet?"

"He sent a text earlier just to say Happy Birthday. We're going to dinner tonight."

"I know. I know." Allie said excitedly. "You're going to an awesome restaurant. You have to get the steak. And they have the best flourless chocolate cake. And I mean the best. It's gooey and thick and, oh man, it's sooo good."

I eyed Allie and almost laughed out loud. I just knew she had a plan up her sleeve. She'd be going to the restaurant early to decorate the table or prime the waiters or something.

By the end of the day, without eating anything, not even one bite, I felt light-headed and a bit sick. As I trudged up the back porch stairs of the Sandfords', I thought about what I was going to wear to dinner. Tights and sweater? Skirt? What would make me look the skinniest?

I could hear Mrs. Sandford singing, as usual, in the kitchen as I entered.

"Surprise!"

Aaron, Allie, and at least twenty others jumped out at me. My synchro teammates (Wanda included), Nathan and some of his teammates, Jax (Podium's snowboarder famous for his crazy stunt videos), a few of Aaron's hockey friends including Kade Jensen (a good friend of mine from Toronto), and some of the soccer girls.

Tacky, twisty, colourful streamers hung haphazardly from the ceiling of the kitchen and a big Happy Birthday sign stretched between the two side walls. Tons of balloons bounced on the floor. Tied to one of the chairs floated a big Happy Birthday helium balloon, the kind you buy at the supermarket checkout.

But the funniest thing in the entire room was a Pin the Tail on the Donkey game that was crookedly stuck on the wall.

"I can't believe this!" I laughed.

Allie stepped forward. "Tell me you're really, honestly surprised."

"I am," I replied. And I was.

Mrs. Sandford, dressed in her favourite apron, smiled at me. "They've been working on this for a good week." She gave Mr. Sandford her evil-eye stare. "I thought Mr. Sandford was going to say something just the other day. I had to kick him under the table."

Mr. Sandford waved his hand in front of his face. "I wouldn't have said anything."

"It was all Aaron's idea." Allie threw her arm around Aaron's shoulders. "Well, except Pin the Tail on the Donkey." She put her hand to her mouth and giggled. "That was my idea. We got it at Walmart."

"Thanks, you guys." I gave Allie a big hug.

Then I hugged Aaron. Everyone in the room oohed and

aahed so we immediately pulled apart.

"Who's in for Pin the Tail on the Donkey?" asked Aaron. "I'll set up a championship. We can play a round robin." Aaron waved a piece of paper in the air.

"Let's eat first," said Allie. "Mrs. Sandford has it all ready."

Mr. Sandford put up his hand. "I want in. And I'm going to kick some butt."

Everyone laughed and Mrs. Sandford turned and said, "Good grief." Then she pointed to the table, which was stacked with paper plates. "Okay, kids, grab a plate. I have spaghetti, ravioli, chicken, and two different types of salad. All organic."

Allie leaned into me and whispered, "And you should see the cake. So yummy."

"I'm going to change," I whispered back. "I'm in my sweats."

She grinned, a really big grin, and I looked at her suspiciously. "What's that for?" I asked.

"You'll see," she sang. Then she pushed me toward the hallway.

While everyone was getting their food, I snuck through the kitchen. I grabbed Aaron by the arm and said, "I'll be right back. I'm going to change."

He grinned too. "Good idea."

"Okay. You're acting all weird like Allie."

"Hurry up. Or you'll miss the tourney."

I quickly went to my room and shut the door. Then I saw the brightly coloured birthday bag on my bed. I went over to it and read the tag. Scrawled in handwriting I knew were the words: *Carrie. Love, Aaron.*

I reached in and pulled out the gift, wrapped with nicely folded tissue paper and sealed with a little sticker. I carefully peeled back the sticker and unfolded the tissue to see a beautiful aqua-blue, sleeveless silk top. I held it up. The V-neck had a loosely draped ruffle that flowed from the V down.

"Knock-knock," Allie said, rapping on the door, then walking in.

"Did you help him buy this?" I asked.

"Isn't it gorgeous!"

"It's beautiful. So soft."

"Put it on."

I slipped my T-shirt off and put the silk one on.

Allie whistled through her teeth. "Whoa! Sexy mama. Aaron is gonna be in heaven when he sees you. I'll pick your jeans." In one stride, Allie was rummaging through my closet, tossing clothes around like they were basketballs.

I turned and looked at myself in the full-length mirror. I almost gasped. What I saw, I hated. All I could see were huge boobs. My face heated. I wanted to cry. I looked so fat.

Allie threw me a pair of jeans. "Here, throw these on with it."

I whipped the silk shirt over my head. "I can't wear it."

"Are you crazy, girl? It looks fantastic."

I shook my head. "I just can't." I put my T-shirt back on.

"You know how long it took for him to buy that for you? The guy hates shopping. And he paid a fortune."

"I don't care."

Allie stood with her hands on her hips. "What's wrong?"

"Nothing. I just can't wear it, okay? It shows too much cleavage."

"It doesn't show *that* much cleavage. Anyway, you're lucky you've got cleavage. I've got two pancakes with one chocolate chip each."

"Just go back to the party. I'll be out in a minute."

"Do you want to talk about something?" Allie asked softly. "You've been acting funny lately."

I sat on the end of my bed and lowered my head. My eyes welled up.

Allie sat beside me.

I sighed and wiped my cheeks. Then I said, "Susan pulled me off the top of the lift, told me I needed to lose weight, and she said it in front of everyone." I shook my head and exhaled through my mouth. "And now they're all out there, in the kitchen. I can't wear something that makes me look fat. They'll all be talking about me tomorrow. Especially Wanda."

"That's so nasty! Your coach needs to be smacked up one side and down the other. That's not right. No wonder your sport has so many screwed-up athletes. And what do you care what Wanda thinks?"

"Aw, let's face it. I have put on weight since I went on the pill last spring." I looked at Allie. "I just wish Susan hadn't said so in front of everyone. I can't have acne again. I don't want to go through hiding my face behind my bangs and never looking at anyone because I think they're staring at my zits."

"I hear ya."

I attempted a smile for Allie's sake. Sure, she had never had a zit in her life, but last spring when the doctor recommended I go on the pill, she totally got how I felt about my acne. She said it was how she had felt her whole life being African-Canadian and six feet tall; everyone was always staring at her.

"What are you going to do?" she asked.

"Lose the weight. It's my only option. I don't want to lose Aaron."

"He's not going to break up with you 'cause of acne."

"He might."

"How much you want to lose?"

"Ten pounds."

"That's a lot."

"I know."

"Promise you won't start throwing up. 'Cause that's gross and disgusting."

I held up my pinky finger. "Promise." I paused before I said, "And you have to promise me that you won't say anything to Aaron about this."

She winked and looped her pinky finger with mine. "Gotcha." Then she stood. "Come on, let's get some dinner." She lifted her eyebrows. "The cake is flourless. No carbs."

After Allie left my room, I rewrapped the top in the tissue, put it back in the bag, and stuck it in the far corner of my closet. Maybe when I lost weight, I'd be able to wear it. I put on the jeans Allie had picked out and then pulled out a big, baggy sweater to wear overtop.

When I entered the kitchen, Aaron glanced at me, and I immediately saw the crushed look on his face. I walked over to him and whispered in his ear, "I love it. I just don't want to spill spaghetti on it."

"You really like it?"

"Like it?" I answered. "I just told you I love it. Thank you." I squeezed his hand and he squeezed mine back.

Then he leaned over and whispered, "I'm going to win at the Donkey game."

I playfully slapped him. "Why does everything you do turn into a competition?

"I need to get pumped for North Dakota." He leaned into me. "Let's get some cake."

"Sure," I replied.

Cake had so many calories whether it had flour or not. I touched his arm. "I should talk to Mrs. Sandford first. You get cake. I'll get some later."

CHAPTER FIVE

Thursday, November 18, 6:30 a.m. 126 pounds. Still the same. Didn't eat cake last night. Faked it and threw it in the garbage. Freaking out. Audition is December 12.

One egg, one piece whole wheat toast. 144 calories. All I can have until dinner.

At the pool, I dressed in my black bathing suit and white cap. We all had to dress the same for the figures part of the competition and were given a number so there could be no bias in the judging. We had two compulsory figures to do, and then the judges would draw two more from six potential figures and we had to perform whichever ones were given to us.

"I'm so nervous," whispered Amy.

"I know I'm going to have dry lips," I said. "I used Vaseline."

"Me too. I put it inside my mouth too, to hold my dumb smile." She smiled and I could see that some of the shiny Vaseline had gotten on her teeth.

After warming up on land with stretching and exercises

like jumping jacks, we warmed up in the pool, practicing on our own. Then we all had to line up in single file in the order of our numbers. I was in the middle of the pack.

I shook my legs as I waited. No one spoke. When it was finally my turn, I dove in the water and swam in front of the five judges. I waited patiently, smiling the entire time, the Vaseline keeping my smile in place, as they got organized. Finally they looked at me.

"Porpoise." This first figure, a challenging compulsory figure, was announced.

I submerged. The porpoise required me to go upside down and twist with both legs up and out of the water. Once I completed the figure, I broke the surface of the water to wait for the next figure to be announced.

I completed my next two figures, which I thought I did fairly well. Then it came time for the last one.

"Dolphin."

Great, I thought, *I love this one.* I had always had good flexibility in my back to perform the dolphin arch.

When I was finished, I smiled at the judges, then swam to the side of the pool. I watched as a volunteer gathered all my five marks and walked them around to a table on the opposite end of the pool. They would drop the highest score and the lowest score, and average the three middle scores. I got out of the water and waited for my final mark.

When I heard the 8.8 called out, I balled my hands into fists and whispered, "Yes!"

"You did awesome," said Amy in the change room.

"Thanks," I replied.

"Geez, I wish I could break 8.0."

"You will."

"Yeah, whatever." She waved her hand in front of her face. "Who cares about a figures test? It has nothing to do with Vegas." Then she leaned into me and whispered, "Did you see Wanda flirting with Nathan last night?"

"Hel-lo. Everyone saw. It was so obvious. Allie thought it was hysterical. Wanda was almost drooling over him and Nathan was using his lacrosse moves to duck away."

"I don't think he knew what hit him. Man, she can be aggressive."

"He told me the other day he didn't even know who she was. So I don't think he likes her."

Amy glanced over my shoulder, then whispered, "Here she comes."

"Fun party last night." Wanda took off her bathing cap and tossed her hair. "Even if we did play Pin the Tail on the Donkey."

"That was the best part," said Amy. "Jax got so dizzy he almost fell in the cake."

"That guy is nuts. He combined his Native dance moves with spinning in circles," said Wanda. "No wonder he got dizzy."

"He's not nuts. He's super talented," I retorted. Jax was such a great guy.

"Oh, please. Who would run a snowboard down a little tiny rail and think that was fun?" Wanda tilted her head and ran her fingers like a comb through her hair.

"He speaks highly of you too," Amy said, scrunching up her face at Wanda.

"Talk about crazy," I said, easing the tension. "How about when Nathan pinned the tail in Allie's hair? Now *that* was funny."

"I think Nathan likes Allie," said Amy nonchalantly.

"He doesn't like Allie," snapped Wanda. Then she stalked off.

"You're mean," I said.

"Nope." Amy chucked her goggles and cap in her bag. "She's just getting what she deserves. She's evil."

After I left the pool, I headed straight to the airport to pick up my mom, who was arriving to watch my team competition tomorrow.

The first thing she did when she saw me was give me a big hug. "I've missed you so much," she said, stroking my hair.

"Me too." I hugged her back hard, loving her arms around me.

When we pulled apart, she said, "How did you do today?"

"I got an 8.8!" I punched the air with a fist. I had really missed her today when I'd scored my personal best — usually she was there to cheer me on.

"Honey, that's fantastic!"

"Thanks." I paused for a moment, tilted my head, and took a good look at her. "You look awesome," I finally said. "Did you get your hair done? I like the colour."

She puffed her ash-blond, shoulder-length hair with her hand. "Do you really like it? I went one shade lighter."

"Looks great. I like the cut too."

She put her hand to her chest. "Thank you. I was so

worried about it. Thought it might be a bit short."

I laughed. "Nothing to worry about. You look ten years younger."

"You are way too kind."

I grabbed my mom's bag off the conveyor belt and we headed to my car. Well, our car. She had given it to me to take to Calgary and had bought herself a little beater to drive around Toronto, telling me that she didn't need a good car because she could use the subway.

"Brr. It's cold." She tightened her scarf and took her gloves from her coat pocket. "How's school?" We walked quickly to the parking lot.

"Good." I had to smile. She always asked me that question.

"How's Aaron? You're still with him, right?"

"Yeah, I'm still with him. He's fun. He's at a tournament for a few days but said he'll come to the competition on Sunday. Hopefully he remembers, so you'll get to see him then."

"Has he seen you swim before?"

"No." I shook my head. "He doesn't know anything about synchro."

"He's in for a surprise. I'm anxious to see your numbers. Especially the one done to 'Stairway to Heaven.' I love that song. Reminds me of when I was young. Your dad and I used to —"

"Mom," I said, cutting her off. "I'm not on top for the highlight anymore."

Her brows furrowed. "Why? You got such a good mark in figures today, so you must be improving."

"I dunno. Susan wanted to give someone else a try."

"How *is* Susan?" Mom wasn't fond of my coach. She

called her cold and unapproachable.

"She's okay. I have to admit she does have great choreography. And she does challenge us." We were near the car and I unlocked it with the remote.

"As long as you like her, that's what's important. But Mindy, your old coach, she's not." Mom hoisted her bag in the trunk. Shutting the trunk, she said, "I'll drive. And I'm taking you for dinner."

I got in the passenger seat of the car. I'd only had breakfast but wanted to stay below a thousand calories. I could have salad and maybe a bit of chicken. Or maybe I could have salmon with nothing on it, depending on where we went for dinner. Salmon was expensive though.

"Earth to Carrie," said Mom.

"Sorry. I was thinking about tomorrow."

"How's the Keg sound?"

"Is it too much money?" I eyed Mom. I knew it cost my mom a lot to fly out to see me. I really appreciated her allowing me to come to the school even though I knew she was lonely in Toronto without me. For so many years, it had been just us at home.

She put her arm around me. "I wanted to tell you in person. I got a raise."

"Mom, that's awesome."

"We're celebrating."

We entered the restaurant and the hostess guided us to a table in the corner. Mom and I chit-chatted about everything, but nothing really important. I ordered the leanest steak on the menu, nixed the potato, and asked for lots of other veggies.

"Are you dieting?" Mom asked me as she ripped off a hunk of sourdough bread, the same bread I had passed up. The fresh, warm bread smell wafted through the air along with the scent of garlic.

"More like watching what I'm eating. I just want to lose a few pounds." I leaned back to get away from the tantalizing smells and sat on my hands so I wouldn't be tempted.

She carefully put her bread on her side plate, and looked right at me. "Remember what I've always said . . ."

"I know, Mom."

"You start dieting like some of those other girls and I'll pull you out of Podium and there'll be no more swimming."

"Sometimes I wonder why I tell you things." I blew out an exasperated sigh. "You exaggerate everything."

"Rebecca Johansson got so thin she had to be hospitalized and Sarah Barry had heart —"

"Mom! Stop."

Silence hovered over our table. Mom picked up her knife and buttered her bread. When she put her knife back on her plate, the clang interrupted our silence but only for a second. It returned like a dark prairie cloud. She took a small bite of the bread and chewed it thoroughly before she finally asked, "How many is a few?"

"Ten max."

"Okay. No more than that."

"I have to do it for the Vegas audition I told you about."

"I understand." Then she gave me her serious mother gaze. "But I'm going to repeat, remember what I've always said about —"

Fortunately the waiter arrived with our meals at the

exact moment she was going to give me her standard lecture one more time. Why did parents always have to drive a point home over and over? I felt relieved the waiter interrupted her speech.

I stared at my plate. My steak looked huge. I cut it into tiny pieces so it would take longer to eat. Maybe I'd fill up faster that way.

Partway through our meal, Mom said, "I have something I want to talk to you about."

Uh-oh. Her tone didn't sound good. "What?"

"Your dad contacted me."

I bit my lip and looked away, shaking my head.

"He wants to see you," she continued.

Gritting my teeth, I turned to stare her down. "I don't want to see him."

"Carrie, it isn't good for you to shut him out completely."

"How could you bring this up the day before I compete?" I threw my napkin on the table so it covered my plate.

"I thought that since we had some time alone, this would be a good time. And I waited until after your figures."

"Well, it's never a good time. And you just ruined a great day. I don't want to talk about him and I don't want to see him. He will never ever approve of anything I do."

"I think he's trying to change."

"Ha."

"One day you are going to have to resolve this."

"No, I won't. I talk to him and he'll trash-talk me and control me again. Can you imagine how he'd react to seeing me this fat?"

"Fat? You're not fat, Carrie. And honestly, you're exaggerating. Your father's just trying to reach out."

"I refuse to believe that. He's manipulating you, Mom."

She sighed and then looked at my plate. "Are you not eating anything else?"

I sat back and crossed my arms. "Nope. My stomach's upset now."

In the car all the way to the Sandfords' house, my mom tried to fix the damage she'd done by talking about shopping. She wondered if I needed new jeans or any school clothes and thought we should hit Chinook Mall after the competition because she'd heard they had some great new stores. I softened a bit. I could never stay mad at her for long, and she didn't bring my dad up again.

I was not going to let him control me ever again.

CHAPTER SIX

The next morning my alarm went off super early. I had to be at the pool by seven. Mom would come later with Mrs. Sandford.

In the kitchen I boiled some water so I could mix the Knox gelatin to paint on my hair. Once I had the gelatin mixed, I took the bowl to my bedroom. First I put my hair in a tight bun that sat in the middle of the back of my head. With a small paintbrush, I slathered on the gelatin. Then I grabbed my blow-dryer and heated my hair to make the gelatin shine.

Before I left my bedroom, I searched my bag to make sure I had all my competition pieces. When I had checked each one off my list, I pulled out the scale from under the bed.

When I stepped on it, I groaned. *No!* I'd gained the pound back.

On my way out the door, I took a boiled egg from the fridge.

When I got to the pool, my teammates were in the change room and the makeup was spread out on the bench.

We worked as a group, doing each other's makeup, making sure everyone looked exactly the same. Amy had been designated the makeup captain. When we had a competition, Susan assigned a captain for every job.

Our team suits were black on the bottom, white and silver on the top. When I looked at myself in the mirror, I thought I looked awful. The light top accentuated my boobs.

Amy came up beside me to adjust her silver hairpiece. "Did Susan say anything about your mark yesterday?"

I couldn't answer her right away because my legs looked twice the size of hers. Finally I turned away from the mirror. "She said good job."

"Time for warm-up," yelled Wanda.

"Susan should have made you team captain," whispered Amy.

"One thing Wanda is good at," I replied, "is being team captain. I'll give her that much."

"Yeah, you're right," conceded Amy.

Once in the pool area, we gathered on the deck to do our land warm-up. For thirty minutes we stretched to get limber. Then we dove into the smaller pool, usually the diving area, to swim some laps and practice our moves. After that we had time in the bigger pool, the one we'd be competing in, so we could figure out our walls. Hitting a pool wall meant marks off, so we had to be aware of the pool layout.

"That looked good," said Susan when we were finished pool practice. "I'm pleased." She looked at her watch. "You'll be up soon, so stay warm."

Finally it was our turn. With heads held high and shoulders back, we headed out in single file from the deck to the side of the pool. When we were on our mark, we struck our pose and remained frozen. "Stairway to Heaven" started. One by one we dove into the water, quickly moving to our formation.

When it was time for Amy to do the lift, I swam to where I was supposed to be as the pusher, and sculled in the water so she could get on my shoulders. I lifted her out of the water and she jumped, did her Russian splits, and performed a perfect dive.

At the end we all smiled for the judges, five technical and five artistic merit, and then we swam to the side and got out of the pool.

When we heard the 9.0 called out, we kept our composure until we were back in the change room. Then we broke loose and cheered.

"That's the highest mark we've ever received!" Amy slapped my hand.

"You did a great dive. Wow. It was perfect." I sat on the bench and leaned my back against the wall. "I'm pooped."

"I couldn't have done it without your help." Amy tore off her hairpiece. Then she sat beside me and pulled out a bag of food. She handed me a homemade granola bar. "You want one? Only natural sugar."

"It's okay. I've got a bunch of food too."

"I can't wait for our duet tomorrow," she said.

"Yeah, me too." Amy and I were duet partners and had been working hard on our routine.

Wanda stood on the bench. "Great work, girls! It's

confirmed — we're swimming in the finals on Sunday. Everyone has to be at the pool by 8 a.m. Good luck to all duets tomorrow."

I stood under the shower for half an hour trying to get the gelatin out of my hair. The warm water trickled over my body and I put my hands on my stomach. I was beginning to like the feeling of being hungry.

I met Mom out by the pool where she was sitting in the bleachers. "That was fantastic!"

"Thanks." I grinned.

Mrs. Sandford leaned over and said, "Well done, Carrie. Mr. Sandford said he would come to your duet tomorrow and your finals on Sunday."

I had to chuckle. "Are you dragging him here?"

She waved dismissively. "No. He wants to come."

Mom patted my knee. "Your dad said he wants to see you perform again too."

I held up my hands. "Stop. No more about him."

Saturday, November 20. 124 pounds. Lost three. Trick is to eat breakfast and nothing until dinner.

Amy and I performed our duet and actually got a decent mark of 8.4. Wanda and her duet partner, Crystal, managed to top us with an 8.7. On the way out of the pool, Susan stopped me.

"Your duet had a few rough spots," she said.

"Yeah, we kind of messed up the Barracuda."

"That's okay. The team number did really well. I think you girls can win."

"I agree. It's a great number." I paused for a second before I said, "I really love the choreography."

"Thank you, Carrie. I appreciate your support. And your opinion matters to me."

I shifted my stance and swung my bag a bit. "I better go. My mom is waiting for me."

"How's the food plan?"

"Good," I replied. "See you tomorrow."

Sunday, November 21. Still 124. Once I'm done competition and my mother is gone, I can get back to running.

For finals in synchronized swimming, we do the exact same routine, only the judges have cut more than half the teams. When it was time for Amy's lift, her splits weren't as high and her dive wasn't perfect.

"What happened?" Wanda asked her in the change room.

"I don't know. I didn't get the height, so the dive was off."

"It's all right, Amy," I said. "It doesn't hurt our chance for Nationals."

"Susan will be ticked," said Wanda. "We could have won."

"It's okay," I said. I felt so sorry for Amy. Her face had that crestfallen, I'm-so-crappy look.

Wanda turned to me. "Did you lift her high enough out of the water?"

"I was as high as yesterday," Amy said adamantly. "It's my fault. Not anyone else's."

"Wanda, it's over," I stated. "We'll make it better next time."

"Yeah, you're right," she said. "And now that it's over and we don't compete until January, we can all just concentrate on the audition." She buoyantly lifted her shoulders. "December twelfth can't come soon enough for me. You still going to audition?"

I yanked off my bun holder and threw it in my bag. "Yup."

After showering for forty-five minutes to get the gelatin out, I met up with Mom, Aaron, Allie, and Kade outside the pool area. Aaron and I were always trying to set Kade and Allie up but they seemed to just remain friends.

"I didn't know you guys were *all* going to be here," I said, a little embarrassed.

"I kind of had to come," said Kade. He jerked his head toward Aaron. "He made me."

Allie jabbed Kade in the ribs. "You're not supposed to say that." Then she turned to me. "Girl, I don't know how you stay underwater for so long. I would for sure get water up my nose."

"Me too," said Kade. "How do you go upside down?"

"Ha ha," I said. "We wear a nose-clip. You should try it sometime. It takes strength. You hockey players think you're all sooo strong."

Of course, after saying that, Kade had to flex his biceps. "I think I could do it."

Allie gave him a playful push and he fell into Aaron and we all started laughing.

"I've got an idea," said Mom, basically butting in on the conversation and physical antics. "Let's go eat somewhere. All of us. My treat."

"Wow. Thanks so much, Mrs. Carrie. I'm in," said Kade. "I'm starving."

"Mrs. Carrie?" I laughed, but while I was laughing, I was thinking that I didn't want to go eat. Geez, why did everybody always want to eat?

"There's an Italian restaurant down the street," said Mom.

"Sounds awesome," said Aaron.

When we were seated in the restaurant, I immediately opened my menu. I read it closely, trying to see if there was something that didn't have too many calories. The pressure of reading the menu gave me a pounding headache. The waiter brought a basket of bread and butter, and my mom picked it up and passed it to Aaron first. I watched as the basket went around the table, and when it got to me, I took a whole wheat roll and put it on my side plate.

"What are you having?" I rubbed my shoulder up against Aaron's.

"Baked lasagna."

"I think I'll do salad."

When my salad came, I was glad we were eating Italian because the only dressing choice was vinegar and oil.

"You want the oil?" Allie dumped some on her salad and passed it to me.

"Nah, just vinegar is good."

She narrowed her eyes.

I ignored her. "Hey, did any of you guys see *Glee* last week?"

"I love *Glee*," said Kade, helping himself to another roll.

"You would," said Aaron. "Did you see the Flames beat

the crap out of the Oilers last night?"

The banter about television and sports and everything and anything continued until our meals came. I pushed my food around my plate while everyone dug in and ate like they'd never eaten before. I felt my mother's gaze from across the table.

"I ate some of Amy's homemade granola bars," I said to her.

"As long as you're sure you ate something," she replied.

"Yeah, I did. Don't worry, Mom. It's all under control."

CHAPTER SEVEN

Friday, November 26. 122 pounds. Five pounds! In one week.

"What do you want to do tonight?" Aaron asked at lunch. I had run in the morning because we had a morning off and I'd wanted to get it over with.

"I don't know. We could go to a movie, I guess."

"Or . . . I think Nathan's playing lacrosse tonight. We could go to his game."

"Okay," I replied. "Is it at that arena on 16th Avenue?"

"Yeah, Kade might come too."

"I'll talk to Allie then." I tapped my nails on the table. "I wish those two'd figure out that they should be together."

Since Aaron didn't have a car, I picked him up. Jordan, the little boy he billeted with, greeted me at the door while gobbling down a mini chocolate bar.

"Hi, Carrie. I'm still eating my Halloween candy."

"You must have got tons." I tousled his hair. "Halloween was almost a month ago."

"Yeah, tons." His scrunched his face into a frown. "I

think Aaron's been eating some of it though."

I laughed. "I bet he's been stealing it."

Jordan frowned even more. "He hasn't been giving some to you, has he?"

I thought about the little chocolate bars that Aaron had been eating and offering to me but that I'd been denying. I shook my head. "Aaron hasn't given me one single chocolate bar."

Jordan put his finger to his mouth. "Shh. I'll give you one if you don't tell Aaron."

I clapped quietly. "Oh, goodie."

Jordan bolted up the stairs to his bedroom and within seconds returned with a little Kit Kat bar. When he handed it to me, I so wanted to open it and eat it. "Thanks," I whispered. "I'm putting it in my purse so Aaron can't see."

"Yeah, don't tell him." Jordan shook his head like a dog wagging its tail.

"Don't tell me what?" Aaron clumped up the stairs from his basement bedroom.

"Nothing," I replied. "It's a secret."

"Yeah, Aaron, it's a secret."

After Aaron roughhoused with Jordan for a few seconds, we said goodbye and went outside. The weather had changed in the past few weeks, turning very cold, and there had even been snow. I was used to snow from living in Toronto, but Aaron was a Vancouver boy.

"It's freezing out." He shivered under his thin jacket.

"If you wore something a little heavier, you might not be cold." I slung my arm through his.

"I don't own a real winter coat." He looked down at me

and we stopped for a moment to kiss, his mouth moulding with mine.

"I have an idea how I can warm you up," I whispered, sliding my arms under his jacket and around his body.

"Oh yeah? And what would that be?" Aaron whispered back, his warm breath misting on my skin.

"The Sandfords are out tonight. Until late, they told me. After the game, we could go back to my place."

"All right. Let's leave at halftime."

I playfully punched him. "We can't do that."

"Okay, but let's hope there's not a lot of penalties so we can get out of there early."

"Okay, but you promise not to go eat somewhere after the game."

"Yeah, I promise."

Nathan's team won the lacrosse game. As promised, Aaron and I said our goodbyes and left as soon as the game was over, even though Kade and Allie were waiting for Nathan and going out for something to eat.

We ran to the car, trying to avoid the cold, laughing the entire way. My car was parked right beside Wanda's. She was getting in it just as Aaron and I, hooting and hollering, arrived at mine. She looked over at me and smiled.

"That was a good game," she said.

"Sure was." I nodded.

"Are you guys going out with Nathan now?" She quizzed.

"Not a chance," said Aaron. "Not tonight."

I giggled and Wanda looked at me funny. "We can't

tonight," I said. "I think Nathan's going out with Allie and Kade, though."

"Would you, um, know where they're going?" Wanda jingled her keys.

"I don't," I said.

"Me neither," Aaron said. "I can't believe how cold it gets at night."

"We gotta go, Wanda." I opened the car door, got in, and fired up the engine.

"Why was she asking you those questions?" Aaron said as he rubbed his hands in front of the heater.

"She likes Nathan. And Allie told me that Nathan thinks she's stalking him. It's so funny."

When we got to my place, the Sandfords' car was still gone. Aaron and I went into the house and straight to the living room and the flat-screen television. The grandfather clock, sitting in the corner, chimed ten times. "They won't be home until eleven," I said. "Let's put on *Glee*. I recorded it the other night." I waited for Aaron to make a fuss about watching *Glee*.

"And get under a blanket." Aaron fished one out from the hassock sitting in front of the couch. "If you warm me up like you promised, I'll watch *Glee* with you."

We nestled underneath, and as Aaron wrapped his arm around me, I snuggled my head into his chest. My body seemed to just flow into his and I loved the feeling of his hockey-hardened muscles and strong arms. Everything about him warmed me up, made me quiver, and made me happy. His fingers traced my stomach and then found their way under my shirt. Skin on skin, we connected.

We watched television in silence for a few minutes, with him running his fingers up and down my bare skin. Then he kissed the top of my head. I turned to look up at him and we kissed.

When we stopped to get some air, he whispered, "I'm not cold anymore."

"Me neither," I whispered back.

He continued to run his fingers over my skin, moving them higher and higher. I wondered if he noticed my weight loss. If he did, he didn't say anything and instead moved so he was leaning over me, our faces within inches of each other. I let him gently push me down on the sofa and I wrapped my legs around him.

We hadn't gone far when we heard the sound of tires in the driveway. Aaron and I jumped up.

"They're home early! I'll turn on the lights," I said.

"I'll put the blanket away," he said.

Saturday, November 27. 121 pounds. Lost another pound! Buying new jeans today.

Frost covered the grass and my breath fogged outside my face as I ran to my car, wishing I had an electric car starter — we don't use those things in Toronto. The leather on my car seat was freezing. But the car started anyway, and I rubbed my hands together, watching the temperature gage. "Come on," I whispered.

Without waiting for my car to warm up, I shoved it in gear and drove away from the curb. It took me twenty minutes to get to where Allie waited for me outside the best jean store in the mall.

"Hey girl," she said. "You and Aaron ditched us last night."

"Yeah, we just went back to my place."

"Empty house?"

"Yuppers. You guys go eat?"

"Yeah. And that psycho teammate of yours showed up."

"Wanda?"

"Yeah, she just strolled in by herself and joined us. She pushed herself between Nathan and Kade so she was almost sitting on Nathan's lap."

I laughed. "Nathan's so weirded out by her."

"You should have seen the look on his face. Too funny."

"He claims she's a stalker."

"After last night, I might agree."

"Hey, since you don't like Kade, why don't you try to hook up with Nathan? Then he doesn't have to deal with Wanda."

"He's almost a foot shorter than me!" Allie leaned her arm on the top of my head. "This is what we would look like. Anyway, who said I don't like Kade?"

"Actions speak louder than words."

"Okay, okay. He's just so immature sometimes. Come on, let's get some jeans."

After scouring the racks, I picked four pairs of jeans to try on, all different sizes, and the salesgirl put them in the dressing room for me.

"You find anything?" Allie pushed my curtain aside just a bit and peeped in. When she saw I was dressed in one of the pairs of jeans, she ripped the curtain open all the way. "Come on out."

I stepped out of the dressing room, then looked at Allie and began to laugh.

The jeans she had on only came to above her ankles.

"Are you going to hem those and wear them as shorts?"

"Not funny. But hey, I did find another pair that are long enough. Give me a sec and I'll put them on." She went into her stall and stripped down without closing the curtain. She jumped to tug up the zipper, and when it was all the way up, she opened her arms. "Ta-da!"

"You are so skinny."

"And you got an ass." She turned around and wiggled her butt. "I'm the black girl and you're the white girl and you have the ass." She turned back to face me and eye me up and down. "You've lost weight though. You look a whole lot skinnier."

"It's noticeable?" I did a little dance.

"Yeah."

"Aaron hasn't noticed."

"He's a guy. What do you expect? Get those jeans."

"Yeah, I will. Let's go pay and get out of here."

Back behind my curtain, I stripped off the jeans and slipped on my black tights and long shirt that covered my butt. Did I still have a big butt? I hadn't worn jeans in a long time because none of them fit anymore. I picked up the ones Allie told me to buy and hung them back on the hanger. Then I took the exact same jeans in two sizes smaller and left the dressing room.

We were walking out of the store with our purchases when Allie asked, "Lunch? I'm starving."

"I ate a massive breakfast," I lied. "But I'll walk around

for a bit."

"O-kay. Most people eat three meals a day, you know."

I walked a few steps before I said, "Did I tell you my dad wants to see me?"

"Did he *call* you?"

"Yeah, right." I swung my purchase as we strolled. "My mom said he talked to her. He wouldn't have the guts to phone me. Not after our last blowout."

"Do you know what he wants?"

"Probably to tell me how great his new kid is."

Allie stopped still in the mall, grabbed my shoulder, and spun me around. She stared at me. "You didn't tell me they had the kid."

I tucked my hair behind my ear and glanced away. "I guess it's not that important."

"Boy or girl?"

"Boy."

"So you have a brother?"

I straightened my shoulders, holding my head high. "I will never, ever, accept him as my brother. It's her kid."

"That so sucks." Allie put her arm around me and we started walking again.

And just like that, my shoulders caved in. "I don't care," I said. "I've never been good enough for him anyway, so he had to have another kid with a skinny bitch who hates me. Well, I hate her too. And him, for that matter."

CHAPTER EIGHT

Friday, December 3. Morning. 119 pounds. Weight loss is slow. I'm only down eight pounds and the audition is in nine days.

Friday, December 3. Afternoon. 119 pounds. Afternoon. I didn't lose any weight and I hardly ate lunch!

Friday, December 3. Midnight. 119 pounds. Nothing and I didn't eat dinner!

"Have you lost weight?" Amy asked me after practice on Saturday.

"A little." I leaned against the wall in the change room. My body was tired, really tired. It had been a long practice today with lots of cardio and choreography. A headache pounded in my temples.

"It shows."

I glanced at Amy, and when I saw her sincerity, I attempted a smile and replied, "Thanks."

Suddenly Wanda was standing in front of us. She always seemed to appear like a chinook wind, out of nowhere.

"You guys going to Nathan's Christmas party?"

"Yeah, I think so," I said. I still hadn't moved. "It's the Friday after the audition, right?"

"He invited me!" Her eyes lit up and she grinned from ear to ear.

"He invited everybody," snarled Amy. Then she turned to me. "I'm flying home for Christmas the next morning. But I'm going to go for sure. I'll probably still be drunk when I board the plane."

"Yeah, I'm flying out the next day too," I said.

"It's at the perfect time." Wanda did a little hip-hop dance as she spoke. "Celebration time for making the cut at the Vegas audition. We'll probably have heard by then." Her ponytail swung back and forth before she turned and walked away.

"She is so sure of herself," said Amy.

"Watch. She'll probably make it."

Monday, December 6. 118 pounds. Down one more.

Tuesday, December 7. 118 pounds. Still.

Wednesday, December 8. 118 pounds. And holding. I'm getting frustrated.

Thursday, December 9. 117 pounds. I did it! Now can I drop one more before the audition?

Thursday, December 9. 117 pounds. No change. Cut another 200 calories.

Friday, December 10. 116 pounds. Audition Sunday. Saturday — no food.

Sunday, December 12. 116 pounds. Today's the day. I guess this is it. 116 pounds.

I arrived at school early so I could register for the audition. A table was set up in the school hallway outside the pool, and already the lineup was almost out the front door. Swimmers had flown in from all over Canada for the audition. The hall buzzed, vibrating with a weird, incredibly nervous energy.

My stomach twirled and spun and twisted and somersaulted and did everything possible to make me want to throw up. My pulse raced, my palms glistened with sweat, and my knees shook. As each girl finished registering, I moved up the line until I was in front of the desk.

"Name," said the girl working the registration desk.

"Carrie Munroe."

She asked for more details, phone, address, email, then pushed a piece of paper in front of me. "Could you check to see if your information is right?"

Once I had done so, she handed me a number. "Wear this on the front of your T-shirt for the fitness test and the front of your bathing suit for your pool audition. Now move on down the line to get weighed and measured."

Sweat beaded on my forehead. My mouth was so dry I could hardly swallow as I stepped on the scale.

"One seventeen," the woman doing the weighing announced. Another girl wrote down my weight. I had put on a pound? I had just weighed myself before I left home. Why did I eat the egg yolk? That was just plain stupid.

As I stood to get my height measured, the girl behind me in line stood on the scale.

"One hundred and eight," said the woman doing the weighing in.

I wanted to cry. The girl was nine pounds less than me and at least one inch taller.

In the change room, I found a small spot on the bench to get dressed into my shorts and T-shirt. With my head bowed and my hair in front of my face, I snuck a glance around the room. Everyone looked so skinny and tall, and I didn't see any of my teammates. I snatched a hair elastic out of my bag and stuck my hair in a ponytail. Without looking at anyone, I headed into the gym to warm up.

Once registration was done, the organizers of the audition came into the gym and called out numbers, which divided us into groups. Then the fitness component of the audition started.

I waited my turn, watching each girl in front of me do their beep test, or multi-fitness test, running as fast as they could from one line to the next, then back again, touching the floor every time. The lines were only twenty metres apart, and the test was like a super-fast shuttle. By the time it was my turn, I knew what I had to beat.

"Go!"

I started running. Back and forth. Touching the floor and sprinting again. And they counted. I kept going. I had to do this.

By the end of the entire gruelling fitness component,

which also included sit-ups, push-ups, chin-ups, vertical jumps, and burpees, I thought I was going to pass out. Stars swam in front of my eyes. My lungs burned with every breath I took. My stomach ached and I swore the egg was sitting in the back of my throat.

And yet I felt like I'd done really well. I headed back to the change room to put on my swimsuit and bathing cap.

"I hate that beep test," said Amy, puffing beside me. "I was out of breath from running 'cause I was late getting here, then I was the first one up. I thought I was going to barf."

"Me too," I said. "Glad it's over."

"I wonder what we'll have to do in the pool."

"Your guess is as good as mine."

Swimmers dressed in all different colours and styles of bathing suits milled around the pool deck, shaking their legs, stretching, and jogging on the spot. I stretched my legs and hopped back and forth.

One by one they called the swimmers to a private area that had been blocked off with black curtains. When it was my turn, I inhaled and walked behind the curtain to stand in front of a panel of judges. My throat clogged and my heart raced.

They eyed me up and down. Did they hate my fat body? I wanted to run. Leave the audition. But my feet stayed glued to the floor. Finally a woman spoke.

"We will put on a piece of music and want you to im-provise a dance on land. Then we will do the same thing in the water."

I waited for the music, and as soon as it came on, I start-ed to move. I have no idea why I picked the moves I did.

I just listened and danced, ignoring the panel in front of me, ignoring the stares burning my body, just remembering moves from all the dance classes I had taken in the past. When the music stopped, I looked up. The judges were writing. I tried to catch my breath.

"Now in the pool, please." The judge spoke in a clipped tone.

I slipped on my cap and nose-clip, dove into the pool, and waited until I heard the music. Then I performed in the same way, forgetting about everything but the music. This time it felt good to be surrounded by the water.

Then I was dismissed. I got out of the pool and made my exit.

Once in the change room, I sat on the bench. My legs shook like crazy and my heart was still beating through my skin. That had been the most nerve-racking thing I had ever done. I leaned my head against the wall, and my mind started analyzing each and every move I had done. What had possessed me to think they were good? Had I lifted my leg high enough? My thoughts bounced in my head like a rubber ball and I wanted it to stop.

After a few minutes, I opened my eyes. *Enough,* I thought. I stood and decided to shower, get dressed, go home, and just forget.

Fifteen minutes later I was ready to go. Amy was just coming in.

"I was so bad." She looked like she might cry. "I couldn't think of anything to do in the improv, so I did the same thing over and over."

"Don't worry. I'm sure we all did the same."

"Well, it's over. Nothing we can do but wait. They said the email will come this week, telling us if we got a call-back" Amy pulled out her towel.

"From what I gathered," I said, slinging my bag on my shoulder, "you only get an email if you get selected."

"Have they set a date for the next round yet?"

"Not an exact date, but they said sometime in early January. And it will be in Vegas."

"That's one email I won't be getting," she moaned.

I patted her on the back. "Don't be so sure. You were probably better than you thought." I left the pool, trying not to think about what I had and had not done.

That night, my mom called to find out how the audition had gone.

"No idea," I said. "It was kind of weird. We just improvised."

"Do you think you did *okay?*" Mom asked.

"I don't know. I just moved to the music. I was a lot shorter than some of the girls."

"But you're strong. And that is a huge component for synchro. You have to stop thinking that your body is not right. Look at how successful you've been. Maybe they're looking for girls who look like you."

"I doubt it, Mom. You should have seen the skinny girls."

"Carrie, your body is not going to hold you back."

"How's everything in Toronto?" I changed the subject.

"Good. I think I might get another promotion."

"That's great. We can celebrate when I come home at Christmas."

"Speaking of Christmas, your dad phoned again. He was hoping to see you before Christmas. He's going to be away on Christmas Day because they're going to be in the Caribbean for a week and they're leaving Christmas Eve."

"How stupid," I retorted. "They're taking a new baby to the Caribbean."

"The baby will be over three months old. I travelled with you when you were that age."

"I don't want to see him before Christmas. It's always on his schedule. Everything is always about him and we have to adapt. Tell him he either sees me Christmas Day or he doesn't see me at all."

The line went silent and I let the silence linger. My blood was boiling. I wanted to throw the phone against the wall. *He* couldn't see me on Christmas because *he* had plans, but *I* was supposed to change *my* plans to accommodate him. Well, it wasn't happening.

"You're being unreasonable," said Mom softly.

"No. I'm. Not. He's being controlling. Tell him to forget it. I'll see him next Christmas when he's home and has time for me." I waited a beat, then said, "I gotta go. I got tons of homework to do."

I pressed END on my phone and fell back on my bed to stare at the ceiling. I had only met my dad's new wife twice, and both times she had stared at me as if I was some overweight piranha. And she had spoken to me in that condescending, want-to-be-a-good-stepmother voice. As I sat there fuming, my phone rang. I checked the number, and when I saw it was Aaron, I answered.

"Hey," he said.

"Hey." I propped myself up on one elbow. Just the sound of his voice made me relax.

"Did you kill it today?"

For the first time all day, I laughed. "Aaron, I'm not sure I *killed* it. But I did okay. How was your game?"

"We killed it. We won 7–1."

"That's great."

"You still want to go to Nathan's party on Friday?" he asked.

"Yeah, do you?"

"For sure. It should be good. Everyone's going." He paused momentarily. Then he said, "Maybe we should get some alcohol. Vodka?"

"I'm not going to drink." Alcohol had way too many calories.

"It's Christmas. No one will find out if nothing crazy happens. I don't think there are that many people going."

"I'm still not drinking."

"Okay," he said, "that's cool. You can be the DD."

I hung up the phone and tossed it on my bed. Then I got up and went to my closet, flinging open the door. I pulled out a black sequined dress I had worn last year for Christmas. When I tried it on, it looked awful. Hanger after hanger, I tried on all my good clothes, but nothing looked good. I slipped the last dress off my body and stood in front of my mirror in my underwear.

Fat.

CHAPTER NINE

Monday, December 13. 116 pounds. Eight more to go to get to 108. And sixteen pounds to get to 100. I want to hit that 100 mark. My new goal.

Tuesday, December 14. 115 pounds.

Wednesday before synchro practice, everyone was talking about Nathan's party. No one mentioned the audition anymore, because now it was a waiting game.

I put on my suit and cap and went into the pool to warm up. After my laps, I got out of the pool and saw Amy jerk her head toward the pool entrance. "Uh-oh," she said.

Immediately I turned to see Susan and Tracy hauling in the scale. "Before-Christmas weigh-in!" yelled Susan.

The moans and groans circled among the girls as we all gathered around the scale.

Susan looked down at her clipboard. "Carrie."

My heart rate escalated and I stepped forward and onto the scale. Tracy fixed the weight, and when it balanced, Susan announced, "One sixteen."

"Good work, Carrie," said Susan. "You've lost the ten. You've reached your goal."

When practice was over, I was towelling my hair when I heard my phone beep. I pulled it out and read a text from Aaron asking if I wanted to get together. I texted him back, saying sure but just for homework. Then I noticed that I also had a couple of emails. For the past three days, I had been checking my emails to see if there was one from the audition. They had told us they would let us know in the next few days.

Immediately I opened my file, and when I saw an email from the Vegas Company, I almost freaked out. My hands shaking, I pressed OPEN and read: "*You have been selected to attend the synchronized swimming callback auditions in Las Vegas on January 15. We will be in touch with the audition details.*

Shocked, I muttered, "I got in." I said this more to myself than to anyone else in the room.

"You what?" Amy came up behind me and looked over my shoulder. Discreetly, I showed her my phone.

"Omigod! Congrats!" She gave me a hug. Then before I could tell her not to say anything, she shrieked, "Carrie got a callback!"

I shook my head but of course it was too late. The girls who had email on their phones were frantically searching through their bags and pockets and purses.

Wanda clicked on her phone and scrolled and scrolled. Then her eyebrows furrowed and her mouth sagged. She tossed her hair, shrugged, and put her phone on the bench.

"Maybe it's delayed," I said to her. "My phone does that sometimes."

"Yeah, maybe," she said softly. Her face flushed and her eyes glazed over. She picked up her phone again and took another look. Then she put it in her bag.

I left the change room holding my phone tightly in my hand. As I was walking by Susan's office, I heard her call my name. I peered into her office and she was sitting at her desk.

"Come in." She motioned for me to enter her lair.

When I was standing in front of her desk, she said, "You've lost a lot of weight. That must have taken extreme willpower."

"I've been following your food plan," I lied.

She tilted her head and squinted a little, like she was assessing me. "I want you to add some calories. I think you're losing too much too fast."

Something inside me bristled. She had put me on the plan, or at least thought she had, and now she wanted to change it just when I was seeing success.

"Sure," I answered.

"Good." She picked up her pen and I knew I was being dismissed.

I was almost at the door when she said, "Oh, and by the way, Carrie, congratulations. I heard the good news about the Vegas audition."

I stopped moving and pivoted so I was once again facing Susan.

"I knew of all my girls, you could do it," she said.

"Thanks," I said sincerely. "I think the weight loss helped."

"I'm sure it did." She nodded once. Then she leaned forward and interlaced her fingers. "But . . . be careful. Too much too soon can be dangerous."

As I walked down the hall toward the front door of the school, I called my mom. "I got a callback!"

"Honey, that's terrific."

"I'm going to have to train over Christmas. I'll phone Mindy today and ask her if I can come to the pool. I have some stuff I want to work on."

"That's a great idea. I'm so proud of you. I can't wait to see you when you arrive in Toronto on Saturday. I'm so glad you have the full two weeks for Christmas."

"This is going to be the best Christmas ever." I stepped outside and the cold wind blasted my face.

"Carrie, we should talk about your dad," Mom said.

I stopped, letting the wind swirl snow around my face. "Are you freaking kidding me? You're mentioning Dad after I just told you my good news? Not again, Mom. I told you how I felt."

I shoved my phone into my pocket, pulled up the hood of my parka, and ran to my car.

Thursday, December 15. 115 pounds. Down one more. Only seven to go for Vegas. Christmas = calories = willpower. Bought a size zero dress. Can't eat today. Dress must fit for party tomorrow night.

"I don't have anything to wear to the party," said Allie in physics class. "And I don't have cash to buy something new. I just bought jeans. Speaking of jeans, you've never worn those new ones you bought."

"Wear your black dress," I said.

"I'm so bored with that dress." She slouched in her seat and tapped her pen.

"I'll accessorize it for you." I winked at her. "I've got the perfect jewellery. We'll make it look great. And I'll do your hair."

"Okay," she conceded.

I was about to say something more about what would go with Allie's dress when Aaron sat down in the desk beside me.

"Hey," I said.

"Last physics class before holidays!" He flipped his pen in the air, catching it between two fingers. "I can't wait to be finished."

"We were talking about Nathan's party," I said to Aaron. "Is Kade going?"

"I don't think so."

"He's booked to fly out tomorrow," Allie piped up.

"You come with us, then," I said to Allie. "I'm driving."

"Yeah, come with us," said Aaron. "It's going to be fun."

"You guys don't mind?"

"Absolutely not," I answered. "Let's get ready at my house."

Suddenly the drone of the teacher's voice began and we all turned to face the front.

At last physics ended, which meant we were all one step closer to Christmas vacation.

Susan made our afternoon practice extra tough. She said we were all going home to stuff ourselves and she wanted us to leave on a good note. I made it through the practice but was so tired at the end, and my head was pounding again.

I was walking down the hallway toward the front door of the school with my head down, feeling as if my feet were caked with two inches of mud, when I heard someone call my name.

I froze. A man's voice. I swear my heart stopped beating and fell to my toes.

My body shook, my breathing sped up, and my skin itched. Bile rose in the back of my throat.

I swallowed and closed my eyes. I felt the urge to run away. And fast. But I couldn't. My feet were stuck. My breath came out in small gasps. It was him. Why was he here?

Finally I opened my eyes and stared down the hall toward the door and the voice.

My father stood just inside the school by the front entrance with his hands tucked casually in the pockets of a knee-length black coat.

As soon as he saw me staring dumbfounded at him, he unleashed his hands from his pockets and strolled toward me. The soles of his dress shoes squeaked as he walked.

"Carrie," he said again.

How dare he surprise me like this? How dare he? I turned my head but just until I composed myself. Then I turned back to glare at him. "Why are you here?"

"I was in Calgary on business and I wanted to see you before Christmas."

"How thoughtful." Sarcasm laced my words.

"You look good, Carrie." He smiled, showing a mouthful

of perfect bleached teeth. "Really great."

I laughed, hysteria seeping through the loud ringing in my ears. "You're dressed like a GQ model, I'm in grey sweats, and you're telling me I look great. I get it. Now that I'm thinner, you want to have something to do with me. Now I make you proud."

"Carrie, come on. Let's not start off this way. Let me take you to dinner. We can go somewhere nice. We can talk."

"About what?"

"Your mom told me about your audition. Congratulations."

Again I laughed, but it didn't sound nice. "I thought you hated synchronized swimming. Thought it was a 'silly' sport." I used my fingers to make quotation marks. "Why the change of heart, Dad? Because finally my fat little body did something good with my silly sport?"

"Please, Carrie. Let's not go back in time. Why don't we just go forward?" My dad gave me his best smile. Phony, as always.

"Like you have with your new wife? And baby. Congrats, by the way."

He clasped his hands, and for a moment, I nearly caved in. There was almost something soft in his hand movements, something gentle in the slump of his shoulders. "Having him has made me want to make things right with you."

Don't get sucked in. Don't.

"Oh, I see," I said. "Your new son gets your love now." I paused. "And I get it almost seventeen years later?" I started to push forward.

As I brushed by him, he put his hand on my shoulder. I cringed. I hated how he always tried to touch me as if he cared. "Please, let's go to dinner." He was almost begging. "Or even for a coffee. I have a Christmas gift for you. I think you'll like it. Your mom suggested the idea."

"Mom?"

"Yeah, we talked about me coming to see you."

"I can't believe this!"

I pushed by him and broke into a run, my tote flapping against my side, my parka slung over my shoulders. And I didn't look back. Not once.

When I reached my car, I was panting and sweating and shaking even though I wasn't wearing my jacket. Hurriedly I unlocked it and jumped in, starting the engine and backing out before letting it warm up. I peeled out of the parking lot, my tires squealing. Tears fell down my face. How could he have just shown up like that? Why didn't my mother warn me? They set the meeting up behind my back. I bet he only wanted to get in touch with me now because I had lost weight and accomplished something with my synchro. That was the only reason.

I kept driving but not in the direction of the Sandfords'. I actually had no idea where I was going. I just drove. Then in front of me I saw the golden arches of McDonald's.

I yanked on the wheel and headed to the drive-through.

"Two Big Macs, two fries, and a large coke," I said through my tears to the voice at the drive-through ordering window.

When I pulled up to the food window, I handed the girl the money and she looked at me funny. Whatever. I got my bag of food and parked in one of the parking spots away from all the lights.

And I ate.

Every last crumb.

Then I opened the car door, put my finger down my mouth, and threw up.

CHAPTER TEN

Friday, December 17. 114 pounds
Egg with no yolk — 17 calories
Veggies – 30 calories
Sugar-free Jell-O – 10 calories

After school on Friday, I went directly home and got into my running gear. I had two hours at least before Allie came over and we started getting ready for the party. I was picking Aaron up at eight-thirty.

I ran and I ran. I tried not to look at my watch. And I tried not to think about my dad, but I wasn't successful. I hadn't phoned my mom yet, because I was so mad at her. Obviously she'd helped plan his visit.

As I ran, I thought about everything. I thought about happier times when I was little and my dad actually liked us, and we would decorate our Christmas tree and drink eggnog and he would hoist me on his shoulders so I could put the angel on top. But then things went sour. He hated me as a teenager. I was too fat. I was in the wrong sport. I didn't get good enough grades. And he hated my mom too.

But that was because of Kelly. I saw them at a restaurant, holding hands and kissing. I was ten and with my friend's parents. I told my mom.

I ran faster.

The shit hit the fan. They'd been having an affair for seven years.

My mom had tried to keep me out of it, but I heard every fight from the top of the stairs.

Finally I rounded the last corner. I slowed to a walk and looked at my watch: an hour and forty-five minutes.

Inside the house, I drank some water. Then I quickly showered.

I was blow-drying my hair when Allie barged into my room. She was loaded down with bags. One was a red, gold, and black Christmas bag.

"Merry Christmas!"

I clicked off my blow-dryer. "Merry Christmas to you too!"

Suddenly my legs buckled and my breathing picked up pace. I grabbed on to Allie's arm so I wouldn't fall.

"Hey, what's the matter?" She held my arm to steady me.

Within seconds my breathing returned to normal so I let go. "I'm just overheated from the blow-dryer. Let me get my gift for you." I opened my closet door to get the box I had wrapped with Santa paper and red and green ribbon. When I pulled it out, a bag of my stashed food toppled to the floor.

Allie immediately bent to pick up the food, grabbing a package of sugar-free candies. "Why are you hoarding food in your closet? Mrs. Sandford has a kitchen, y'know."

I snatched the bag from her and shoved it back in the closet. "It's just some extra stuff." Then I picked up the wrapped box. "You're going to love what I got you." I handed her the box and she handed me the bag.

"Let's open at the same time," I said.

Allie ripped paper and I reached into my bag and pulled out a smaller bag. I laughed. "You wrapped it twice."

"Oh yeah," she said. She had the paper torn off her present and was opening the box.

"They're amazing!" Allie held up the Swarovski champagne earrings I had bought for her.

"You can wear them tonight with your dress," I said. "I told you I'd accessorize that dress and make you the princess of the par-tee."

"They are so beautiful!" Her eyes danced. "Now time for you to open your gift."

I opened another bag and another bag until I got to a really small sac. I pulled the strings and opened the sac, peering inside. "Allie!" I pulled out a silver heart necklace. "It's gorgeous!"

"Dainty, just like you."

We hugged, then suddenly she broke away and said, "We better get moving. It takes a long time to make this hair of mine straight and beautiful." Then she looked at a wrapped present sitting beside my not-yet-packed suitcase. She grinned. "Is that from Aaron?"

I smiled. "Yup. He wants us to open our gifts Christmas morning. Thinks it will be fun if we call each other."

"That is sooo cute. I bet it's clothes. He's gonna love

the shirt you got him."

"Did you help him buy mine?"

"Maybe." Then she laughed. "No more questions. I promised I wouldn't tell." She put her hand to her head. "Now . . . about this hair."

Over an hour later, Allie's hair was totally straightened and mine was down and curled. I took my new, red, size-zero satin dress off the hanger. As I was shimmying into it, Allie said, "You're getting so skinny."

I slid the dress down my body.

"How much you down?" she asked.

"I dunno. Like only ten pounds."

"No more, girl. You'll be nothing."

"Nah. Never." I zipped up the back of my dress, barely getting it done up.

When I turned to look in the mirror, all I could see were boobs. They were squished into the red dress, making my cleavage huge.

"Love the dress," said Allie. "Where'd you get it?"

I didn't want to see boobs anymore so I turned from the mirror. "Wow, those earrings work."

Allie twirled her head, making the earrings swing. Then she said, "Let's go. Aaron will be waiting."

Aaron *was* waiting. He wasn't wearing a suit, but rather a nice pair of black pants and a grey dress shirt.

"Wow," he said when I walked into the front entrance, his eyes widening. "You look hot."

"Thanks." I smiled. "You too."

Before we left, he grabbed his backpack and I knew exactly why he was taking it. Inside, zipped in a little pocket, would be his alcohol. This would be his first time drinking all fall.

Noise from the party could be heard from outside as we walked up the steps.

"Sounds packed," said Allie.

Nathan greeted us at the door. He was wearing a black suit, white shirt, pink tie, and black fedora. "Come on in," he said. "Looking good, Scary Carrie and Allie-bean." He slapped Aaron on the back. "In the kitchen, mate."

A beautifully adorned Christmas tree shone brilliantly in the front room, the little white lights shimmering in perfect harmony. Red, green, and gold ornaments sat in festive bowls. Other ornaments were placed around the house. I had a warm, fuzzy feeling as we made our way through the crowd to the kitchen. Nathan was one of the lucky athletes at Podium who lived at home.

Obviously tonight, his parents were out, since bottles of booze sat like tall city buildings on the island in the kitchen, with red plastic glasses lining the counters. It was risky to have a party with booze, but if nothing went wrong and nobody showed up that wasn't from the school, we all knew it would be okay. The kitchen buzzed with a no-more-school-for-two-weeks energy.

"Allie, you want a drink?" Aaron asked.

"Ah, maybe one." She pinched her finger and thumb together. "But a little, little one. You know me, I'm not a drinker."

"Sure," said Aaron. Then he turned to me. "You want a pop?"

"Only if it's diet," I answered.

My stomach growled and I felt really light-headed as I followed Aaron, weaving my way through the bodies in the kitchen. Plus, I could feel a headache coming on again.

"Hey Carrie," said Amy. She had a drink in her hand. "Cheers. Merry Christmas." She held up her red cup. Then she leaned toward me. "Wanda is following Nathan everywhere," she whispered. "It's so funny."

"By the end of the night, there will probably be a blowout between them if Nathan drinks enough," I said.

"Hey, who was that man you were talking to yesterday?" Amy sipped her drink.

My heart thudded to a stop. I didn't think anyone had seen us by the front entryway. "No one," I said. "At least no one important."

Just then Aaron handed me a red cup. "Here." Then he said, "I'll be back in a sec."

Just as he left, someone pushed me from behind and I lunged forward, splashing Diet Coke on my bare chest.

"Sorry, Carrie," said Jax.

I laughed. "No biggie." I patted my chest.

Then a guy behind Jax said, "If I'd just done that to her, I'd offer to lick it off. She's got a great rack."

Jax pivoted, his long black ponytail spinning with him, and said, "Shut up." Then he turned back to me and said, "Sorry, that guy's a jerk. You look really nice, Carrie."

My face flushed with an unbearable heat. I looked at Amy and said, "I'm going to the bathroom."

"Sure," she said. "The guy *is* a jerk, you know."

I locked myself in the bathroom and looked at myself in the mirror. My boobs were like inflated balloons. How could I have worn this dress and thought I looked good? I sat down on the toilet seat. Did every guy on the planet think of me that way? I felt sick, yet kind of buzzed in a weird way, even though I hadn't had anything to drink. And my head was really pounding now. Maybe I should have one drink. But no, I was the DD tonight, so I couldn't. What I needed was an Advil or Tylenol for my headache. And perhaps I should go home, get changed, and come back. I'd worn the wrong dress. Or just stay home. As I ruminated, someone knocked on the door.

"I gotta pee." The voice was a girl's.

I opened the door and in flew a beautiful, dark-haired girl. Before I could leave, she shut the door, sat on the toilet, and peed. "Who are you?" she said, a glazed look in her eyes.

"Do you go to Podium?" I was totally confused. I'd never seen this girl before and she had me in the bathroom with her while she peed. So weird. It might have been easier if she wasn't absolutely gorgeous and skinny to boot. Why was everyone skinnier than me?

"Not a chance," she said. "I'm here with Ryan from the lacrosse team."

"I'm leaving." I put my hand on the doorknob.

"Wait till I finish." Then she stood up and flushed the toilet. "Done." She moved to the sink to wash her hands and I took that as my cue to leave.

I had my hand on the doorknob when she grabbed my arm. "Hey, you look like you could use something to give you a lift." She pulled a little container from her purse and shook out a tablet. "You want one? No calories."

Visions of my father flooded my mind. He hated drugs and had always told me to leave them alone. Just like he had always told me to leave food on my plate and not eat candies or ice cream and to wear clothes that covered me. My hand reached out like a claw. I wanted something to make me have a good time at this party, take my headache away. I didn't want to be a Debbie Downer all night; it wasn't fair to Aaron or Allie or Nathan.

"They're super mild," said the girl. "Just little uppers. They make you happy, nothing else."

"I'm driving," I said. I'd never done anything like this before but I knew some swimmers took pills to stop them from eating.

"You eaten much?"

For some reason, I felt some sort of freaky bond with this stranger. "Enough," I said.

"Gotcha." She winked and nodded. "With no food, it'll hit you right away and it'll wear off in an hour or so. By midnight you'll be great."

"And you promise no calories?"

"Oh, I promise. That's a must for me."

"Me too," I said. "Okay. Thanks."

I took the little blue pill from the palm of her hand and stuck it on my tongue. Then I swallowed.

CHAPTER ELEVEN

By the time I left the bathroom and returned to the party, the noise had escalated and the bodies had multiplied. I looked for Aaron and spotted him across the room with Nathan and a few other guys. I made my way over.

Partway there I started feeling a bit fuzzy and giddy, also warm and sweaty, which was weird because lately I'd been cold all the time. When I finally reached Aaron, I was hot but feeling happy. The girl had been right. If I stayed like this for an hour, and if this was all the little pill did, then I would have fun at the party without having a drink. No calories. I giggled.

"Hey," said Aaron. "How you doing?"

I giggled again, unable to stop myself. "Good. I'm really good." Then I turned to Nathan. "Great party."

He held up his glass. "Merry Christmas."

"Yeah, for sure," I replied. "I need a glass to hold up."

Aaron frowned at me, just a little. "Did you have a drink? Don't forget, you're driving."

I shook my head and the movement made me dizzy. The room seemed to blur, all the bodies meshing together like in one of those photos taken with strobe lights in the background. I laughed uncontrollably. I could hear music coming from the living room, speakers pounding out the bass.

"I'm gonna dance," I said.

I jostled and weaved my way through the crowd and finally got to the living room, where the furniture had been pushed aside to create a dance floor. The girl who gave me the pill was dancing as well, and she waved at me.

"How you feeling?" she asked when I reached her side. She had to yell over the loud music.

"Excellent!" I replied. I started to gyrate to the music.

"You go, girl!" she said.

I continued to move, bumping and grinding to the beat of the music, unaware of people around me. I threw my head back and shimmied. I had my eyes closed when I felt a hand on my arm.

When I opened my eyes, I saw Allie looking down at me. "What are you doing?" she hissed.

"Dancing." My body didn't stop moving, not for a second. I had no idea how long I'd been dancing.

"You got your dress hiked up to your butt and your boobs spilling everywhere."

I glanced down. One strap of my dress hung down my arm and my black bra was in plain sight. I laughed. Like, who cared?

"Come on." Allie grabbed my upper arm. "You need a breather."

I yanked my arm free. "I want to dance some more. This is fun!"

Suddenly a camera clicked. O-kay. They wanted skin, I'd give them skin. I started dancing again, flinging my head back and shaking my boobs, the straps of my dress going lower and lower.

"You're out of it," said Allie. "I'm getting Aaron."

"Look at Carrie, everyone!" I heard Wanda yell.

"Go, Carrie, go!" someone else hollered.

I was going all right. I started swinging my head in circles, making my hair fly all over the place. Maybe I should just take the dress off. I felt so free — until I felt another hand on my arm.

"Stop, Carrie." It was Aaron this time.

"What? I'm not doing anything wrong."

"Let's go outside." He sounded so stern!

I let him pull me out the back door and onto the porch. The cold air blasted me, but I could feel his warm breath sheltering me. I stared up at him and suddenly I felt an urge so strong that I reached my hands up around his neck and kissed him. I wanted him. Right now. Outside on the porch. We'd never done it before. Maybe tonight was the night. I pushed my body into his and lifted my leg, grinding my hips against him.

He gently pushed me back. "How much did you drink?"

"I didn't drink."

"Carrie, don't lie."

"I'm not."

"We should go home. Just catch a cab."

"How about" — I nuzzled my nose into the curve of his neck — "we go back to my place and sneak into my bedroom."

"Carrie, stop." He pushed me away again. "You're acting crazy."

"You don't want me?"

"It's not that. You're being weird."

I poked his chest. "You're just like my dad. You don't want me either." I couldn't seem to stop what was coming out of my mouth. My head was swirling and everything around me seemed so bright and sparkly. The light from the back porch pulsed and the music from the house pounded. I just felt so free of all inhibitions.

"Why are you talking like this? You shouldn't drink."

"I didn't drink! Now come on, play with me." I swung my hips.

He held up his hands and moved away from me. "Don't," he said.

"Oh, I get it," I retorted. "You think I'm too fat. That's why you don't want me."

I pushed away from him and stormed back into the kitchen. He tried to grab my arm, but I jerked away. I thought I heard him calling after me, but I ignored him. Where was that girl? Maybe she had another pill.

I went back to the dance floor to find her, and when I did, she discreetly handed me another pill, which I swallowed. The music moved me again and I started dancing. A couple of times, Aaron and Allie tried to get me to stop, but I didn't listen. I stayed on the dance floor.

Suddenly, or not so suddenly because I totally lost track of time, I felt a hand on my shoulder. When I turned, I saw Aaron and this time he had his coat on and was scowling.

"It's time to go."

"Aww, don't be a party pooper. I don't wanna go." I put my finger on his lip.

He pulled back and shot me a scathing look. "Everyone is leaving, Carrie."

I glanced around. Had the party wound down already? Yeah, a lot of people had left. What time was it? Where was Allie? Had she left?

"I want to stay," I moaned. "Let's be the last people to leave."

"No. I'm leaving now. If you don't come with me, you can find your own way home. I've given Allie your keys."

"Stay with me." I jutted out my bottom lip and gave my best sexy pout. Then I held up my finger. "One dance and I'll leave."

He spun on his heel and stomped toward the front door. I ran after him in my bare feet. Unexpected tears spilled from my eyes. "Aaron!" I cried. But he kept walking.

He stormed out the front door and I followed, traipsing through the snow. Finally he turned and glared at me.

"I'm going home with Jax," he stated. "Go back inside if you want to stay."

Suddenly I felt dizzy and cold. I wrapped my arms around my shivering body. "Why are you being so mean?" I choked out my words.

"Whatever." Without hesitation, he climbed into Jax's car and it spun away from the curb.

I stood there for a few seconds in the snow, watching the tail lights of the car disappear. Then I ran back up the icy steps and into the house, my feet frozen. Wiping my face, and not looking where I was going, I bumped into Wanda.

"Whoa, Carrie. What's your problem? Oh right, Aaron left without you."

"Shut up!"

"I don't blame him. Who wants a slut for a girlfriend?"

"At least I'm not a stalker!"

"Stalker? What are you talking about?"

"Nathan can't stand you."

"You're such a liar."

I leaned forward until I was inches from her face. "He doesn't like you."

"You're drunk." She pushed by me and I toppled onto a little table in the foyer, sending a basket of Christmas cards to the floor. They spilled everywhere.

Dizzy, I grabbed onto the wall. When I looked at Wanda, I saw double. Her face moved in and out. Had she really just shoved me aside? A rush of adrenalin flowed through me and I shouldered her, sending her crashing against the wall.

"What is wrong with you?" she screeched as she tried to keep her balance.

"You pushed me first!"

"I was just trying to get by."

"You are such a liar."

"First I'm a stalker. Now I'm a liar."

"Nathan knows you lied to me. He doesn't like you." I knew I was hysterical, but I couldn't stop myself from spewing angry words at Wanda.

"Why are you doing this?" Wanda asked. "And why do you care?"

"OMG." My head was spinning and my body floating.

"Nathan's my friend. That's why I care. Get it through your head — he has no use for you!"

Without a moment's hesitation, she reached for me, grabbed a fistful of my hair, and yanked. The pain ripped through my scalp. I screamed and slugged her in the stomach.

"Cat fight!" I heard someone squeal from the distance.

"Holy crap, this is a good one! Carrie and Wanda are going at it!"

"Carrie, stop!" I heard Allie's voice yelling from the distance.

Then I felt a pull on my forearm. "Carrie, don't, please." I turned to see Nathan, his eyes wide with panic. "My parents are going to freak if they come home and find that something bad's happened. The party wasn't supposed to be this big."

For a second I couldn't breathe. I gasped and held my hand to my chest. What was I doing? This was not me. I saw Allie in the crowd of gawkers, staring at me. She shook her head. Disappointment was etched into her face. I put my hands to my mouth. That's exactly what I was to my dad: a big disappointment. And now I was to Aaron and Allie too.

Just then I caught a glimpse of myself in the hallway mirror. I quickly pulled up the straps of my dress and wove my fingers through my messed-up hair. Mascara had smeared under my eyes and made me look like a raccoon.

"She started it," Wanda cried to Nathan. "She —"

"Wanda, cut it," Allie snarled as she stepped forward.

Then she put a hand on mine and whispered, "You need to go home."

"Nathan," I said quietly, tugging on his arm. "I'm so sorry." I lowered my head. "I really am." My shoulders shook as I began to sob uncontrollably.

"Hey, it's okay, Scary Carrie." He wrapped his arm around me and rubbed my back. Soothed by his comforting body, I rested my head against his chest and sniffled.

"Nathan, do you want me to get everyone else out of here?" Allie asked.

"Perfect. Thanks, Allie-bean." Nathan continued to rub my back. Then he yelled, "Party's over!"

Again I said, "I'm really sorry. I'm a mess."

"I can't believe this!" Wanda said angrily. "She starts the fight and you're comforting her. Are you sleeping with him too, Carrie?"

"Wanda, just leave," Allie said as she picked up the basket and cards that had fallen off the little table. Then she started to collect cups and beer bottles and pop cans.

"This isn't fair!"

"Go home, Wanda," Nathan said.

As she stalked out the front door, Wanda shouted, "I'll get you back for this, Carrie."

CHAPTER TWELVE

My alarm went off at seven the next morning. I groaned. My flight left at ten. I had to get to the airport by eight-thirty. I got out of bed and almost collapsed on the floor. I grabbed the knob on the top of my bed frame and sat on the edge of the bed, then put my head between my hands. I had always been clean and never done drugs, and now I couldn't say that. I'd taken those pills from that girl. What were they? I had no idea. Why had I been so stupid? I threw my pillow across my room.

Finally, when I felt like I could move again, I crouched down on the floor and pulled out my scale.

Saturday, December 18. 112 pounds.

I stepped into the shower and let the water stream over my head as my mind kept reliving the party. Why had I been so stupid?

I towelled off, then stared at my body in the mirror in my room. I pinched the skin on my stomach.

You're fat.

I dressed in baggy sweats and grabbed my bags. Mrs. Sandford was waiting to drive me to the airport.

"Thanks so much for the ride," I said, getting out of the car at the airport departure level. She hadn't mentioned how late I had come in, and for that, I was truly thankful.

"Make sure you get some breakfast," she said.

She had tried to feed me before we left, but there was little time and I had said that I would get something from Tim Hortons at the airport. "I will," I said. "And you have a Merry Christmas with your children."

She beamed. "Oh, I will. I'm so excited to see them. And you have fun with your mom and grandparents."

I nodded, trying to fake being happy when really I was incredibly miserable. After checking in, I went through security and right to my gate. I pulled out my phone and sent Aaron a text. Then I sent one to Allie.

Right away my phone rang and Allie's name popped up on my screen. "Hey," I said sheepishly.

"Have you been on Facebook this morning?" Allie's tone was not exactly warm and fuzzy.

"Thanks for taking me home last night."

"Have you been on Facebook?" she repeated.

"No. Why?" I slouched in my seat and fiddled with the ties on my backpack.

"Wanda posted photos of the party." She paused. "You're in way too many and they're not exactly flattering."

"Do I look fat?"

Silence on the other end. I let it hover. Then Allie said, "There are photos of you half naked and all you care about is if you look fat? What is wrong with you?"

"Nothing is wrong with me. I just asked a question."

"What happened to you last night?" she asked.

"Nothing."

"I'm your friend," she said softly. "Don't lie."

I let out a breath and ran my fingers through my hair. "My dad visited me at school the other day."

"You're not answering my question."

"He pissed me off, so I guess I overdid it."

"You were the DD." She paused momentarily before she asked, "Was he nasty to you?"

"Just his being there was nasty to me." I sighed. "Are the photos that bad?"

"Yup. She's also spreading rumours that you took drugs and that you slept with Nathan."

"That bitch!"

"Carrie, if any of this surfaces at the school, both you and Nathan will be in trouble. The photos are from a party at his house. And you look completely wasted."

"Have you talked to Aaron?"

Silence again. This time, when I let it hover, I did so because tears were cruising down my cheeks and my throat was clogged.

"You're lucky it's Christmas holidays," Allie said quietly. "Hopefully this will all blow over."

"I texted Aaron, but he didn't get back to me." I lowered my head and let my hair fall in front of my face to hide the tears.

Allie exhaled loudly. "Carrie, he might need some time."

On the plane I kept my phone in my hand until the very last moment. No text back from Aaron. I kept checking.

"You have to turn that off," said the airline attendant.

I nodded, clicked off my cell, and shoved it in my backpack. Then I leaned back and closed my eyes, hoping to sleep all the way home.

As soon as we landed at Pearson International, I pulled my phone out of my bag and turned it on. Still no text from Aaron. He would definitely have landed in Vancouver by now. I wished I could see him and talk to him. I hated being so far away.

My mom greeted me and immediately frowned. She could see a problem a mile away.

"Honey, what's the matter?" She held my shoulders and looked me in the eye.

"Nothing," I answered, twisting away.

"Something is wrong. Tell me."

I waited a second, before I blurted, "Why did you tell Dad to visit me?"

She sighed. "I didn't tell him to go. He phoned and asked if it would be all right, and I said he could make that decision."

"You knew I didn't want to see him."

"If he wants to try and reach out to you, that's his choice. I'm not going to stop him."

"Well, because of Dad visiting me, Aaron and I had a fight."

"I'm sorry. I really am. It wasn't my place to tell him not to see you. You're sixteen now, almost an adult."

All the way home, on the busy 401 highway, my mom

asked me questions, which I answered with as few words as possible. When we got home, I hauled my suitcase to my bedroom and shut the door, ignoring the beautiful Christmas decorations that Mom would have spent so much time putting up. I flopped down on my bed with the pink, ruffled bedspread and gazed around at all the familiar things — trophies, medals, ribbons, and photo collages of me with friends from junior high. One, made by my friends in grade eight for my birthday, was titled "The Many Faces of Carrie." I looked so happy. Why couldn't I just be that kid again instead of an almost-adult? For the millionth time, I checked my phone, but there was no text from Aaron, so I sent him another message. Number ten. Surely he would answer soon!

I got off my bed and set up my computer on the desk, logging immediately onto Facebook. There in vivid colour were the photos from Nathan's party. Horrified, I put my hand to my mouth and groaned. When I scrolled down to read all the comments, I saw Aaron's name and his message: "*Remove these photos.*" Other messages slammed Wanda and said to take the photos off, including ones from Nathan and Allie. But then there were those who thought the photos were hilarious.

But Allie had been right. I did look wasted, like a total, white-trash slut, but I also looked like a blimp with my breasts spilling out all over the place. Plus, my face looked bloated, pudgy.

Then it hit me. How was I going to keep my journal without a scale? My mom didn't have one. I couldn't survive without a scale!

A knock on my door made me jump and I immediately logged off. "What?"

My door opened just a little bit. "I thought I'd make us dinner soon," said Mom.

"I'm not hungry. I have to go out anyway."

"Where are you going? To see some friends?"

I tried to fake a smile. "I still have some shopping to do."

"Don't buy me anything, please. I just love having you home. I thought maybe we could go to a Christmas movie this week, like we always do." Her face lit up. "Or I could get us tickets for the National Ballet performance of *The Nutcracker.*"

"Okay," I said.

That one little word made her step into my room, lean over me, and hug me from behind. "Let's make this a good Christmas," she said.

"I'll try," I replied.

That afternoon I purchased a scale and hid it under my bed. Mom tried to feed me, but I told her I had something when I was out. We talked at the kitchen table over tea and everything returned to somewhat normal because I was home and not at school.

Finally, just before bed, I saw that Aaron still hadn't sent a message back. And so I called him instead of texting. Fully expecting to get his voice mail, I was surprised to hear his voice.

"Hey," he said.

"Hey," I replied. "You made it home."

"Yeah."

"How was your flight?"

"Good."

"And is it good to be home?"

"Yup."

I paused, then said quietly, "I'm sorry about last night."

"Did you see Facebook?"

"Yes. Thanks for sticking up for me."

"I didn't do it for you. I did it for Nathan. He could get kicked off his team for having a party where people got totally wasted. Apparently there were drugs too, not just booze — some chick brought them."

"Really," I said.

"And you don't know anything about that?"

I swallowed, trying to moisten my dry throat. "No, I don't. And I said I was sorry."

"I know." He softened a bit.

"Are we okay?" I asked.

There was a massive pause on the other end of the line, like someone had pressed the MUTE button. I waited. Finally he said, "I think we should take a break from each other over Christmas and then see where we're at in January."

"O-kay. But I still want you to open the gift I gave you."

"You too. But I don't think we need to talk until we get back to school."

After the phone call was over, I curled under the covers and cried myself to sleep.

CHAPTER THIRTEEN

Sunday, December 19. 114 pounds. No more tears. More than ever, I need to lose the weight. Aaron doesn't want me, and if the school sees the photos, I could be kicked off the synchro team and out of the school. All I have is my audition.

Two days before Christmas, I went to see my former coach, Mindy. We had always been super close and she was like a big sister and mother combined. As soon as she saw me, she enveloped me in a big hug.

"It's so good to see you, Carrie!"

"You have no idea," I replied.

"How's the school?" She eyed me carefully.

"It's . . . challenging."

"That's a good thing. You need to be challenged. And I don't think you were getting challenged here."

"Yeah. You're probably right."

"Susan, she's known to be a tough cookie."

"That's being nice," I said.

"Well, let's get you in the pool and we'll work on some new moves for your audition." She patted me on the back.

"I'm proud of you for making that callback. Not many Canadians did."

I blew out a rush of air. "I have no idea what it will be like in Vegas."

Mindy shrugged and smiled. "In a few weeks you'll find out. Now get ready. I'll meet you in the pool."

Minutes later, towel in hand, I walked toward the pool. Mindy looked at me funny, her head tilted to one side. "You've lost weight," she said, sounding surprised.

"I needed to."

"Not really," she replied. "What was appealing about you before was your muscle. You could be put in any lift position: flyer, base, or pusher. Being this tiny means you are only going to be seen as a flyer. It's perception."

"I had put on a few pounds being away from home," I said. "I had to lose *some*."

"Well, Carrie, you have been extremely successful."

We got down to business, and it felt incredible to be back in the pool with Mindy because she was so encouraging and helpful and honest, but in a kind way. That night when I got home, I greeted my mom with a sincere smile and I sat down at the table and ate a decent dinner.

Monday, December 20. 115 pounds. One night and I put on a pound. If I keep eating with my mom every night while I'm home, I'll put every pound back on. I used to be able to eat a ton and never put on any weight, and last night all I had was some chicken and rice and veggies. I have to stop. I have to stop.

"You're going for a run this morning?" asked Mom. "It's

Christmas Day. Let's stay in our pajamas and have break-fast."

"I'll be back in an hour," I said. "You relax, take a long bath, and I'll be home before you're out of the tub. Then I'll make you breakfast."

The quiet streets greeted me like a friend. Doors were shut and curtains drawn as most people were still in their houses probably opening presents or eating breakfast. In total zen mode, I ran up and down the city streets, one block folding into the next, one corner rounding to another. I hadn't opened Aaron's gift yet and I wasn't sure I was going to. True to his word, he hadn't bothered to call me, not once.

Ninety minutes later, I jogged down my street, heading back to our small house. When I walked in the front door, I could smell bacon. I thought I would throw up.

"That was a long run," said Mom.

"I walked some."

"I'm impressed. You used to hate running. Why don't you get showered and I'll finish breakfast." Then she started singing "Jingle Bells," and I laughed at her as I headed down the hall.

In my room, I pulled out my scale. If I weighed myself after a run, I was always lighter.

Sunday, December 25. 113 pounds. Yeah, I'm almost there. Only five more till I reach my 108 goal. Then if I'm still fat, I'll try for 100. To survive Christmas Day, I need a strategy. Grandpa can't see very well, so I'll sit beside him. Stay away from Grandma — she'll want to fatten me up. Wear bulky clothes because Grandma thinks everyone should be fat.

I feel so sad today. I want to call Aaron and wish him Merry Christmas. I miss him so much.

Sunday, January 2. 109 pounds. One more pound and I'll be ready for the audition.

"Love you," said my mom. "But see you in Vegas very soon." She pinched my cheek. Mom and I stood just out front of the airport security entrance.

"Yeah, I can't wait."

"Carrie, I want you to really focus on eating well before the audition. You're going to need energy."

"Mom, I do eat." She had been constantly harassing me during the Christmas break.

"You know Mindy agrees with me."

I frowned. "Mindy? When did you talk to her?" Mindy wasn't my synchro coach any longer, so my mom shouldn't be talking to her about me.

"The other day. She's worried about you too."

"There's nothing to worry about." I kissed her on the cheek. "I have to go or I'll miss my flight."

When I got back to Calgary, Allie met me at the airport. Her flight from Halifax had arrived earlier than mine, so she'd offered to wait for me.

"Hey girl! Great to see you!" She hugged me.

"How was your Christmas?" I asked. We headed to the carousel to get my bag.

"Good. Parents spoiled me rotten. My mom fed me the best meals and baked the most amazing treats. How was yours?"

"Good. Pretty quiet. Mostly just me and my mom, though we spent time with her family."

Allie popped up one eyebrow. "No surprise visit from Daddy?"

"He tried when he got home from wherever he was basking in the sun. Wanted me to meet the new little brother, but I said not a chance."

We got my bag off the belt and headed to Allie's car, which was parked outside. I shivered when I hit Calgary's winter air. "Man, it's cold."

"It's not too, too bad," said Allie. "At least it's not thirty below."

We got in the car, and once the car had warmed up, Allie turned the heat on full blast. But even that didn't stop me from shivering the entire way to the Sandfords'.

"What's wrong with you?" Allie asked, glancing away from the road for a second. "You sick or something?"

"I'm just cold."

We arrived at the Sandfords' and Allie said, "Let me help with your bags. Why would you go home with two bags for two weeks? You're crazy."

"I needed to bring some of my winter clothes back and my Christmas gifts. I only went home with one." We yanked the bags out of the car, but mine slipped out of my hand, it was so heavy.

Mr. and Mrs. Sandford greeted me with big hellos and hugs and then Allie and I went to my room. I dumped my backpack on the floor and a few things spilled out, including my journal. I had opened my backpack in the car to get my scarf out and must have forgotten to zip it back up. Allie immediately bent over to pick everything up. I snatched the journal from her hands and stuck it in my nightstand.

"Whoa." She held up her hand. "I wasn't going to read it." She paused. "Talking about Aaron in there?"

"A little," I replied. I sat on my bed and wrapped my arms around my knees. I couldn't get warm even though I had on a fleecy sweatsuit, including a hoodie. And I had a wicked headache. "You talked to him?" I asked.

She nodded and sat on the end of my bed, her long legs stretched out in front of her. "A couple of times."

"Did he ask about me?"

"Yeah." She nodded once.

"What do you think I should do at school tomorrow? I don't know if I should talk to him or not."

She picked at the lint on my comforter. "I'd talk to him."

I hugged my knees in tighter to my body. "So nothing happened to Nathan after his party?"

"Well, he didn't get into trouble with his parents."

"All the photos were taken off Facebook in time then." I rocked back and forth.

"I'm glad Wanda listened to everyone," Allie said.

"She sent me a text and said sorry."

"I hope you accepted. That kind of crap is hard on a team." Allie paused. "I've been a captain long enough to know you can't have infighting."

"I said sorry back."

"Good." She paused again. "You could have gotten Nathan in trouble, y'know."

I rested my chin on my knees. "But I didn't."

"You sound like you don't even care."

"I care, but he's not in trouble, so it's no big deal now."

"No big deal?" She abruptly stood. "You didn't even bother to call him the next day to find out if everything *was* okay."

"Geez, Allie. I was so embarrassed. And I didn't think he'd want to talk to me."

"Girl, you've changed." Allie slung her purse over her shoulder. "I gotta go."

"Thanks for the ride," I said as she slammed my bedroom door.

CHAPTER FOURTEEN

Monday, January 3. 108 pounds. Egg without yolk. 17 calories.

I showed up at school early. We didn't have morning practice because so many girls were flying in and it was the first day back. I was at my locker when I heard Aaron's voice. My heart picked up speed and my hands started to shake. I wanted to turn around but I couldn't, so I just stood like an idiot in front of my locker pulling books out and putting them back to make myself look busy.

"Hey Carrie," he said.

I slowly turned. "Hi Aaron." I was stunned to see that he was wearing the moss green shirt I had bought him for Christmas. I'd known it would look good on him with his dark hair. I hadn't opened the gift he had given me. I'd brought it back from Toronto with me, still wrapped.

"Is it this weekend you head to Vegas?" He awkwardly shifted his stance.

"Actually the weekend after next. I leave on the Friday. My mom will meet me there."

"Yeah, I know. She's excited to be going."

Something twisted inside me and I frowned. "How do you know that?"

He changed his stance again, looking sheepish. "I dunno. I just figured she would."

I wanted to call him a liar, but I had lied to him about taking the pills at Nathan's party and there was no way I wanted *that* to resurface, so I just said, "We better get to class."

We didn't talk much as we walked down the hall, which was just as well because questions raced through my mind. Why was my mom talking to Aaron? *When* was she talking to Aaron? Why didn't she tell me he'd called? That was just totally bizarre.

"Hey, you want to have lunch in the cafeteria?" he finally asked.

"Sure." I smiled half-heartedly. I didn't really want to have lunch with anyone, but if I said no, my chances with Aaron were done.

When I got the cafeteria at lunchtime, Allie and Aaron were deep in some conversation with their heads bowed together. I approached the table, and as soon as they saw me, they both sat up and stopped talking. I sat down. "What are you guys talking about?"

"School. Physics," said Allie. She avoided looking at me. She was a worse liar than Aaron.

I pulled out my bag of veggies and started munching on a cucumber.

"Is that all you're eating?" Allie asked.

"I had a huge breakfast. Mrs. Sandford made me bacon

and eggs and hash browns. And I ate three pieces of toast."

Allie looked at Aaron and something passed between them, unspoken.

Friday, January 7. 107 pounds. I did it! Got to 107 for my audition. Perhaps with all this weight loss, Susan will put me back as the flyer.

Friday, January 15. 104 pounds. Three in a week. Leaving for Vegas.

I packed my bag, and on the very bottom, I put the scale. Once I was sure I had everything I needed, I sat down on the end of my bed and looked at my phone. Nothing; nothing from Allie or Aaron or Nathan or anyone to wish me luck. I threw my phone in my purse. Who cared anyway?

I arrived in the Vegas airport and my mom was waiting for me. I rushed to her, and by the time I did, I was breathing pretty hard.

"What's the matter? You're out of breath."

I put my hand to my chest, feeling my heart fluttering uncontrollably. "I think it's excitement, mixed with nerves."

She flung her arm around my shoulders. "We're staying at the Hard Rock Hotel. It's the one where some reality television show is filmed."

"Mom, the show's called *Rehab: Party at the Hard Rock*. And it's wild, not your cup of tea."

"Oh, I didn't know that." She linked her arm with mine. "Still. Vegas is a great city for a few days."

Outside, the scorching air immediately warmed my skin. I inhaled a deep breath, thinking how nice it was to be out of the cold. Maybe I could finally stop shivering.

"You'll have to get out of those sweats." Mom flagged a taxi. "You must be boiling."

"Not a chance," I replied. "Not coming from Calgary."

Mom and I didn't talk much on the ride from the airport to the hotel, mainly because I was too busy staring out the window at the neon lights and landscape. Massive buildings sat in the middle of a sweltering desert. We arrived at our hotel, and when I got out, the cab driver said, "This hotel has the best pool in Vegas. Have fun, ladies."

In our room after we had emptied our suitcases, Mom asked, "Do you want to go to the pool?"

"Maybe tomorrow after the audition." I lay on the bed, still dressed in my sweats. "I don't think the sun would be good for me today. Too tiring."

"Fair enough," Mom said. "We can rest until dinner."

At the sushi restaurant, which was located right in the hotel, Mom looked across the table and said, "Carrie, eat something. You need energy for tomorrow."

"My stomach is doing flip-flops," I said. "I'm too nervous to eat."

The next day Mom and I caught a taxi to the main strip in Vegas because the audition was at the famous Bellagio Hotel. I swear my feet barely touched the ground when we entered the grand lobby of the Bellagio. Slot machines and gaming tables lined a massive space like cars in a Walmart parking lot. Cards flipped and slot machines dinged over and over. People screeched in joy or groaned in dismay. Mom and I walked the long, wide hallway, dodging people of all shapes and sizes and ages. Some women were dressed in high heels and not much else. Men and young boys wore swim trunks and lame T-shirts, and then there were others who were dressed to kill, their perfume wafting over us. Everything seemed massive and surreal.

I couldn't help but notice that many of the waitresses were skinny with big boobs. Skinnier than me.

When Mom and I finally reached the audition sign-in table, I discovered that there was no weigh-in. We didn't have to line up and check in either, because there weren't that many girls and we all had audition times. This was no cattle call.

I approached the desk. "Hi, I'm Carrie Munroe."

The woman checked my name off the list and then looked up at me over the rim of her reading glasses. "You can warm up to the left of the pool deck. Go behind the black curtain until your name is called."

I did as I was told and put on my suit. First I warmed up on land, then I hopped in the pool. Every ten or fifteen minutes, a woman would come from the other side of the curtain and call out a name. I stopped warming up because it was draining my energy.

Then she came around and said, "Carrie Munroe."

This was it. I followed her lead until I was in front of a panel of people. There were only three this time and I recognized the director of the show from a photo in a magazine.

"Hi Carrie," he said.

"Hi," I replied, not sure what else to say.

"We'd like to see you improv in the water, please. You will have thirty seconds."

I dove in and waited for the music. This time when it started, I tried some of the new moves Mindy had taught me. I swam and moved and performed. The music ended and I lifted my body out of the water and tried to smile, but my breathing was out of control.

"That was good. Thank you. Now we'd like you to do these figures: Full twist, front walkover, porpoise, and dolphin. "

I tried to catch my breath before launching into the figures, but it was hard. I was winded. After I did the four figures, the director said, "Thank you, Miss Munroe. We will send everyone an email."

I was dismissed.

My heart ticked like crazy as I went into the change room and sat on the bench. Shaking, dizzy, I bent over to try to calm my body down. That was it. Over. Now I had to wait to find out. I felt sick to my stomach and ran to the toilet. The only thing that came out was yellow bile.

My mother was waiting for me in the hallway of the Bellagio. As soon as she saw me, she hurried over.

"How did it go?"

"It was okay," I said. "Hard."

She put her arm around me. "I'm sure you did great."

"It's over. I want to forget about it until I get the email."

"Good idea," she said with energy. "We're in Vegas. I think we should take some time to enjoy ourselves. You want to walk around or . . . we could hit the pool." She linked her arm with mine.

"I don't want to go to the pool. I'm tired and I want to sleep."

"Come on, Carrie, let's have some fun. We can't leave Vegas without going to the Rehab pool. You can sleep outside if we go by the pool. We'll find an umbrella."

Back at our hotel, I put on my bathing suit in the bathroom, then I slipped on the hotel robe. I could hear Mom singing in the room. I put my hands on the sink and leaned toward the mirror. *You didn't do well today because you're too fat.*

Mom and I headed into the pool area and found a couple of lounge chairs by the sand that gave the pool a fake beach. I plopped down on one, threw my head back and closed my eyes. The searing sun did feel good on my lids. I rolled my head, opened one eye, and snuck a glance at my mother, who was de-robed, dressed in her bikini, and lying with her head back and her eyes closed. Trying to be discreet, I slipped my arms out of my robe.

"This is the life," said Mom. She turned to look at me. She scanned my body, then her eyes slowly closed and she rubbed her hand to her forehead and sighed.

"What's the matter?" I asked, slipping my arms back into the robe and quickly tying it up.

She smiled weakly. "Nothing."

Later, at dinner, Mom clasped her hands and leaned forward. "Carrie, I'm really worried about you."

I looked away.

"I'm going to be blunt. You're too thin. You're not eating. You are going to damage your body."

"Mom, I'm fine."

"No, you're not fine. I'm pulling you out of the school. And you'll be out of this Vegas show if you don't put on a few pounds."

"You can't do that!"

"I can and I will. I've always told you that if you start dangerous dieting, you are not swimming."

"I'm not dieting dangerously," I snarled. "We talked about me losing a little weight and you said you understood."

"If I remember correctly, you said *ten* pounds."

"I can't believe you're being so mean." I crossed my arms.

"I have a right to be worried."

"I won't leave the school. And I *won't* be taken off a *Vegas* show! And you can't make me. I'm an adult now. Or at least that's what you said when you let Dad visit me."

"Then you have to start eating. Bottom line."

I snatched a roll from the basket and shoved it in my mouth. With my mouth full of food, I said, "Is that good enough for you?"

"Carrie, stop."

"What? First you want me to eat, then you want me to stop. Now you're being just like Dad. Nothing is ever good enough."

CHAPTER FIFTEEN

Mom didn't follow through with her threat, and I got on the plane for Calgary the next day. Now that she was talking to my dad again, about me, she was becoming controlling like him. She just didn't understand. I'd had to lose the weight to have any hope of getting into the Vegas show.

If I made it, she would have to say she was sorry.

The email came two days later when I was in physics class. Shaking, I held my phone in my hand. I had been checking my phone constantly since I'd arrived back in Calgary.

Now, here it was.

"Allie," I whispered.

She looked up and I showed her my phone.

"Why don't you open it?" She spoke with little excitement. "It's what you've been waiting for." Since Christmas we hadn't been hanging out much.

"Not while I'm in class," I replied.

For the rest of the class, I tapped my foot and jiggled my leg and could barely sit still, and I certainly didn't listen to the teacher talk about boring equations. Finally the bell rang and I jumped out of my seat and ran out of the classroom.

The combination of sprinting and nervous excitement made my heart pound. I stood outside the classroom door and my body wouldn't stop quaking as I kept looking at my phone.

"Get it over with," said Allie, sounding almost irritated. "You want it more than anything."

Aaron had also come up and now stood beside Allie.

"You could be happy for me," I said, breathing with great difficulty.

My heart beat. Like rapid crazy. And it wouldn't stop. I put my hand on my chest. It wouldn't stop racing. Everything went blurry in front of my eyes. I grabbed onto Aaron for support but felt myself sliding to the floor. In the distance I heard Allie's voice, "She's fainting!"

My world went black.

I felt something cold on my face, and Mrs. Nelson, a math teacher, stood above me. "She's coming to."

I stared up at all the people peering down at me. I could see Aaron and Allie and Nathan and Amy and even Wanda. "I'm okay," I said. I tried to sit up.

"Okay, everyone off to class," said Mrs. Nelson. "I'll take Carrie to the infirmary." She helped me stand up.

Aaron stepped forward, visibly upset. "Carrie, are you okay?"

I nodded. Maybe he still liked me.

"Call me." His voice almost trembled.

"And me too," said Allie quickly.

My phone. Where was my phone? Frantically I searched the tiled floor. "Where's my phone? Where's my phone?"

Aaron handed it to me. "It's broken. You can't text. Call, okay?"

Mrs. Nelson put her hand under my elbow and guided me to the school infirmary to see the nurse. My legs felt like noodles.

"Mrs. Nelson, I need to get to a computer. Now."

"You have to be checked out first."

Once I was with the nurse, I said, "I've just got my period. And it always makes me low on iron." It was the best excuse I could think of to get out of there and get to a computer.

Just saying I had my period made me think about when I had it last. Way back in November. I knew I wasn't pregnant because Aaron and I hadn't gone all the way yet. I probably didn't get my period because of all the stress in my life.

"I can't let you go after a fainting spell."

"I'm fine."

"If you are, we'll know in a matter of minutes."

After she checked my heart with a stethoscope, she said, "You need to make a doctor's appointment. Your heart rate is high. Too high."

"Okay," I said. I had fainted from stress. But I had to agree to see the doctor so she would let me go.

"Would you like to go home for the day? Get some rest?"

"Sure." I would have to dodge Mrs. Sandford, because she might ask too many questions. Lately she'd been asking me some bizarre things, and she and my mom talked way too much.

"I don't want you to go to practice today," said the nurse. "I'll talk to your coach. I will also phone your parents."

"Mother," I said. "I don't have a dad."

"I'll phone your billet parents to see if one of them can pick you up."

"I can take her." Allie's voice sounded from the doorway.

I slouched in the front seat of Allie's car with my arms wrapped around my body and my foot tapping. Allie let her old clunker car idle in the cold weather.

"You want to use my phone?" she asked.

Nervous pain shot through my stomach. "Sure," I answered hoarsely, my mouth dry.

She handed it to me. "Good luck." Then she put the car in reverse and backed out of the parking spot.

I clicked through all the necessary steps to get to my email as Allie drove down the snowy streets. My hands were so cold I could barely hold onto the phone.

"My car will warm up in a minute," said Allie flatly.

I nodded and kept scrolling until I came to the email. "Okay," I said. "This is it."

I opened the email to read:

Thank you very much for your recent participation. We liked what we saw and will be holding another callback on February 21st. You are invited to attend. Details will be sent at a later date.

"I got another callback!"

"That's great," said Allie.

"You don't sound too excited." I glanced at Allie. She stared straight ahead, obviously not happy for me.

"This whole Vegas thing has changed you," she said.

"Not really," I said. "If you were my friend, you'd be happy for me."

Wednesday, January 19. 102 pounds. 202 calories.

Friday, January 21. 102 pounds. 200 calories.

Sunday, January 23. 101 pounds. 156 calories.

Friday, January 28. 99 pounds. 101 calories. Under 100. They have to pick me now.

Tuesday, February 1. 98 pounds. Egg white. Jell-O, Jell-O, Jell-O. Rice cake. 77 calories.

After practice that morning, Susan pulled me aside. "I'd like to have a chat with you this afternoon," she said.

"We don't have practice," I replied, a bit confused.

"I know. I'd like to meet with you, though. How about four o'clock. In my office."

"Okay." I walked away wondering what was so important that she had to call me into her office. My stomach really hurt and I put my hand on it. Why did Susan have this effect on me?

All day I shivered and my stomach ached, plus I had a raging headache. The minutes ticked by and I got more and more nervous about my meeting with Susan. Maybe she had seen the photos from Christmas? No. That party was history.

At exactly four o'clock, I knocked on Susan's office door. "Come on in, Carrie," she answered.

I took two steps, then stopped. I looked around the room at the semicircle of people sitting in chairs, all staring at me.

"What's going on?" My voice trembled.

I looked from my mom to my dad to Mrs. Sandford to Allie to Aaron to Mindy to Susan and to a man I didn't know. My heart raced. My legs shook. My throat dried. And my stomach screamed in pain. Clutching it, I bent over at the waist, trying to catch my breath. This wasn't happening.

"Carrie, I wanted everyone here," my mom began softly.

I looked up, shaking my head. "Why?"

"You need help."

"Help! With what?"

The strange man spoke up. "Carrie, my name is Dr. Alan Schmidt. Your parents and friends have some serious concerns about your eating habits."

"OMG! This is an intervention! Are you guys crazy? I don't need this!"

"Yes, Carrie, you do." Mom stood and reached her arms out to me.

I stepped away and refused to accept her hug. She sat back down.

"What is wrong with everyone? I got another callback for a Vegas audition and you guys want to do this to me now?"

"I think the best thing to do," said Dr. Smith or Smitt or whatever he said his name was, "would be for you to sit down, Carrie, and we'll go around the room and let everyone talk for a few minutes."

"I don't want to sit down."

"Carrie, please," said Mom.

"Carrie, just sit down, please," begged Allie.

I plunked down on the only chair left, obviously the one they were saving for me, and crossed my arms over my chest. I didn't want to hear what anyone had to say.

"Let's start with friends," said the doctor.

"Carrie," said Allie, her voice trembling. "We used to share everything. Now you hide so much. You have food stashed in your room. And you have a diet journal. You used to be fun and now you won't eat or go to restaurants with us. You've changed and I just want my friend back." Her voice wavered. Tears streamed down her cheeks. "I miss you."

"You read my journal?" Anger erupted and I ejected my words at her.

"Carrie, I'm sorry. I caught a glimpse of an entry in it that day it fell on the floor. I knew then it wasn't an ordinary journal. I had to find out what was wrong with you. I want our friendship back." By now she was sobbing. "This Vegas thing has you out of control."

I lowered my head and pulled my knees up. I couldn't stand to see her cry and I didn't want anyone to see me cry. I didn't want to cry. I didn't want them to get the better of me. They were all just jealous. I pressed my forehead to my knees.

Then I heard Aaron's voice. "Carrie, you have to eat sometimes. What I liked about you when I first met you was how much fun you were and so unlike other girls. I hate seeing you just wasting away. You're a good athlete and you don't need to do this. And . . ." I could hear his voice catch. Was he going to cry too? This was horrible. "Like Allie, I really, really miss you."

Even with my head down, I knew he was holding back tears. Tears started rolling down my cheeks, and I shoved my fist in my mouth to stop them. I refused to look up. He was the one who broke us up. Not me!

"Carrie," said Mrs. Sandford. "You used to be so joyful and carefree and I've noticed such a change in the past few months. We love you like a daughter and only want to see you healthy and happy."

"Carrie," said Mindy gently. "I knew something was wrong at Christmas. And I talked to your mom right away. You are too good at what you do to mess up your chances like this. You don't have to have a body like everyone else. You're not built that way. The reason you're so good is because you always took care of yourself and had so much power and so much passion. You've been successful the way you are . . . the way you were."

I rocked back and forth and continued pushing my forehead into my knees. I couldn't stand this.

"I agree with Mindy," said Susan. Just hearing her voice jolted me and made me look up. I knew I was a mess but I didn't care.

"You told me to lose weight!" I shrieked. "You embarrassed me in front of everyone." I didn't care how loud I was. So what if she kicked me off the team?

Susan sighed. "Yes, I did, and I'm sorry about that. Never again will I do a weigh-in. I didn't want you to lose weight this way. And I only thought you should lose ten pounds to help with your lifts."

"You're just like my dad, always critical. You tried to put me on a food plan!"

"No, Carrie, that food plan is a healthy diet that was supposed to give you the proper fuel as an athlete. I have never had such a talented swimmer before. I knew you were destined for great things and I wanted to make sure they happened for you. I wanted you fuelled the right way. And I was hard on you to give you that mental edge needed in our sport. But my tactics were wrong. Carrie, I'm sorry. We've both learned something here. I take responsibility for my part in this."

"And I take responsibility too," said my dad quietly.

The entire room stilled. The silence eerie. I glared at him.

"Why are you here? You don't care about me!" My words echoed off the walls.

"That's not true, Carrie."

"It is so true!"

"I'm sorry for not being there for you when you were young."

"Oh, don't kid yourself, you were there for me for a while. You were there, but I could never do anything to make you happy. I thought you'd be happy that I was skinny!" My voice had escalated to a scream.

"Right now," he paused to take a breath, "I'd be happy

if we could just spend some time together." His voice was so quiet it was almost inaudible. "I want you to get healthy and be that beautiful, bubbly girl you once were."

"You never gave *me* time! Why should I give you any now?"

"Because I love you." His words were so soft and tender that I stopped ranting to really look at him. My dad was crying? I could hardly bear to look at him. Tears rolled down his cheeks and he looked so pathetic when he wiped his face.

I uncrossed my arms. "You have a funny way of showing love, Dad."

He nodded. "I know. I'm working on that. I'm seeing a therapist. I want my relationship back with my daughter." He lowered his head and then his shoulders started to shake.

I couldn't stand this anymore. I had to get out of this room. I got up to leave, but my mom moved like gunfire and got in front of me. When her arms circled me, I melted, and like my dad, I started to sob.

Then I felt another set of arms around me and I recognized the smell of my dad's cologne. I was still sobbing, letting my body deflate, like a big balloon losing air. They held me for a long time and just let me cry. Then I felt other arms around me, Aaron's, Allie's, Susan's, Mindy's, the Sandfords' — all the people who loved me.

"Carrie," said my mom softly. "We want you to go to a rehab clinic to get over this."

"No," I sobbed. "No. No. No." I shook my head.

Rehab? This was crazy. Was I out of control? Had I taken

it all too far? I wanted the show, desperately wanted it. Maybe I could do it on my own. Maybe I could just start to eat a little bit again and be okay.

"You need help, Carrie," said the doctor. "To do this on your own is too hard."

I wanted to still swim. Be part of a team. Live my dream and be part of a Vegas show. "I can do it on my own," I sobbed. "I know I can. Please, I have to go to Vegas."

"Go to rehab," said my mom. "And let everything just work itself out."

Mindy wiped the tears off my cheeks. "Vegas will always be there for you. You are talented. You have a long career ahead of you but only if you take care of this now. If you let this go any further, your career will be over for good."

Something hit me hard and I grabbed my stomach. Hunger pains shot through me. I wretched. Then I vomited on the floor. Nothing came out but bile. I stared at the floor, at what I had just thrown up. Was that what was left of my stomach? What had I done to myself?

"But more importantly," said my mother, sobbing, her arms wrapping around me, "you might do damage to yourself." She lifted my chin, made me look at her. "Carrie, I can't lose you. I just can't. Please, just listen to the doctors. I'm begging you."

Friday, February 25. 109 pounds. I've put on over ten pounds since being in rehab. I actually liked being skinny and I feel fat again. The therapist said my feelings are normal. From being here, I know I'm lucky I only ate the way I did for a short time. Some girls in here have had eating issues for years, going up and down like yo-yos. So many have tons of medical problems and they might never get well again. These girls go to websites that promote anorexia and bulimia and it's almost like a cult. It's their life. I don't want that life. I want to do synchro still. One girl died when I was here, and that was a real wake-up call for me. I don't want to die. I said goodbye today, and I want to keep in touch with some of them but I'm not sure I will. I missed my Vegas audition. It still makes me so sad. I stayed in my room and cried the day of the audition. But there is a big show happening in Toronto in the summer and the audition is in May. Maybe I can do that instead. Mindy said she'd help me.

Mom and Dad were waiting for me in the lobby of the rehab facility where I had just spent the last four weeks. It felt weird to see them standing side by side.

I hugged my mom but not my dad.

"You look great," he said. He took my suitcase.

"Thanks," I replied.

With my dad on one side and my mom on the other, we walked outside. It was a cold but beautiful sunny day. I inhaled a huge breath of fresh air, happy to be free.

"I want you to see someone to help you through this," said my mom tentatively as if she needed to walk on eggshells with me. "I've arranged an appointment for you back in Toronto, if that's okay?"

"Mom, it's more than okay. I'll go to the appointment."

"I think once a week would be good," she continued. "Just to check in."

"Honestly, it's fine."

"I also talked to Mindy. She'll give you some private sessions."

"Thanks. I want to go back to Podium next year. For grade twelve and grad."

Mom linked her arm with mine. "One day at a time, okay."

We walked to my dad's car, and when we got there, I saw another familiar car parked beside it. Allie jumped out and rushed toward me. Then I saw Aaron get out. He hung back.

"Girl, I've missed you." Allie hugged me. "I hope it's okay that we came here," she whispered. She kept her arms wrapped around me. "But we wanted to say goodbye. If you want us to leave, just say so."

"It's okay." My words came out on a sob. "Thanks for coming. I really appreciate it."

I could hear Allie crying when we hugged. When we broke apart, I whispered, "Don't cry."

"You too." She reached over and wiped my cheek. "I love ya."

"I know. I love you too. I'm going to be okay. I learned a lot. Thanks for seeing me through this. You're an amazing friend."

"Lots of other kids wanted to come too, you know. Like Kade and Nathan too." Her eyes twinkled a bit.

"What's up?" For the first time in a long time, I almost felt normal.

She leaned into me. "We've been hanging out, Nathan and me."

"Nathan? Wow. That's so awesome." Although the news was exciting, it also made me sad. I'd had that feeling before and lost it.

Aaron stepped forward and took my hand in his. I tilted my head and gave him a crooked smile.

"The scarf looks good on you," he said quietly. "I knew the colours would work."

I had finally opened his Christmas gift when I was in rehab. I touched my neck, feeling the soft texture of the red and gold cashmere he had bought me. "Yeah, I really like it. You did a good job picking for me. Both times." We just looked into each other's eyes for a few seconds.

Allie nudged Aaron. "You could kiss her," she whispered.

Aaron looked so awkward that I had to turn away. "It's okay," I said. "We were never into PDA."

"What's PDA?" Dad asked, breaking the tension.

"Mr. Munroe, you don't know what PDA is?" Allie gave

him her famous arched eyebrow.

My dad fiddled with his keys. "I guess I'm not up on teenage lingo."

"You got a lot to learn," said Allie.

He tilted his head back, looking up at the Alberta Big Sky for a second before he looked directly at me. "Yes, I do."

I crossed my arms before recognizing my closed body language, then let them hang limp at my side. "It'll take time, Dad." I attempted a smile.

"Caleb's anxious to meet his sister," he said. "Soon, maybe . . . we could do introductions." He sounded so hopeful.

"Maybe." It was the best answer I could give.

Then I glanced from Dad to Mom to Allie and finally to Aaron. "Hey, I haven't had lunch yet. I think we have time to eat before my flight."

ACKNOWLEDGEMENTS

When I started this book, I knew very little about the sport of synchronized swimming. A huge thank you goes to Emily Brooks for all her help. Emily answered my many questions, read my manuscript and brushed me up on snychro lingo. You're the best, girl. Thanks also to my Lorimer team; editors, design team, sales representatives. You do amazing work. And a special thank you goes to my editor, Carrie Gleason. Carrie believed in this series from day one and has made it come to life. I also would like to thank Jim Lorimer for his trust and commitment to the series. And as always, I have to thank you, my dear reader because without you, I wouldn't be a writer!

ABOUT LORNA SCHULTZ NICHOLSON

Vegas Tryout is Lorna Schultz Nicholson's tenth novel and the second book in her Podium Sports Academy series. Lorna is also the author of seven non-fiction books about hockey. Growing up in St. Catharines, Ontario, Lorna played volleyball, basketball, soccer, softball, and hockey and was also a member of the Canadian National Rowing Team. She attended the University of Victoria, British Columbia, where she obtained a Bachelor of Science degree in Human Performance. From there Lorna worked in recreation centres, health clubs, and as a rowing coach until she turned her attention to writing. Today Lorna works as a full-time writer and does numerous school and library visits throughout the year to talk about her books. She divides her time between Calgary, Alberta, and Penticton, British Columbia, and lives with her husband, Hockey Canada President Bob Nicholson, her son who plays junior hockey, and various hockey players who billet at their home for several months of the year. She also has two daughters who now live away from home; but thankfully, the two dogs and the cat are still around to keep her company while she writes.

"Lorna's books are a great read for kids and their parents. They really help teach the importance of having good values both in hockey and in life."

— Wayne Gretzky

DON'T MISS THIS BOOK!

ROOKIE

" I hated this.

I wanted the blindfold off and this to be over. I had a horrible feeling in my stomach. None of this was me. I just wanted to play hockey. *Stay tough,* I told myself. I tried to breathe.

"Let's execute," spat Ramsey. "

Aaron Wong is away from home, a hockey-star-in-the-making at Podium Sports Academy. He's special enough to have earned his place at a top school for teen athletes — but not special enough to avoid the problems of growing up.

Available Spring 2012

Buy the books online at www.lorimer.ca